PRIMAL
INSTINCTS

VOLUME I

By Nicole Edwards

The Walkers

Alluring Indulgence
Kaleb
Zane
Travis
Holidays with The Walker Brothers
Ethan
Braydon
Sawyer
Brendon

The Walkers of Coyote Ridge
Curtis
Jared
Hard to Hold
Hard to Handle
Beau
Rex
A Coyote Ridge Christmas
Mack
Kaden & Keegan
Alibi (a crossover novel)
Trey

Brantley Walker: Off the Books
All In
Without A Trace
Hide & Seek
Deadly Coincidence
Alibi
Secrets
Confessions
Bounty

PRIMAL
INSTINCTS

VOLUME 1

NICOLE
EDWARDS

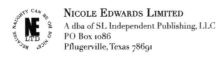

NICOLE EDWARDS LIMITED
A dba of SL Independent Publishing, LLC
PO Box 1086
Pflugerville, Texas 78691

PRIMAL INSTINCTS
Volume 1
NICOLE EDWARDS

COVER DETAILS:

Image: © Emmanma (175652807) | 123rf.com   **Design:** © Nicole Edwards Limited

INTERIOR DETAILS:

Formatting: Nicole Edwards Limited

AUDIO DETAILS:

Image: © Emmanma (175652807) | 123rf.com   **Narrators:** TBD

ISBN: (ebook) 978-1-64418-065-5 | (paperback) 978-1-64418-066-2

BISAC: FICTION / LGBTQ

THE JOB INTERVIEW

Journey Zeplyn

TELL US A LITTLE ABOUT YOURSELF.

What I'm thinking: *This is my first job right out of college, and it's the only one I've applied for because I have an ulterior motive, not to mention a secret obsession with the seedy underground I believe is being covered up by this company.*

What I say: My name is Journey Zeplyn. I was born in Houston, Texas, and lived there until my parents brought us to California when I was twelve. I've spent nearly half my life here, and I can't imagine living anywhere else. I recently graduated from Princeton with a dual degree in Communications and Psychology.

WHY THE DUAL DEGREE?

Thinking: *I get bored easily. Two degrees was the only way to keep me on task. And psychology allows me to delve into the human psyche to figure out why people desire the things they do.*

Say: If you're asking why I chose two different avenues, that's because I have an inquisitive nature. I like to know the why and how of things. That's where psychology comes in. And communications felt like an excellent fit for my creative side.

As for doubling up on classwork … well, I'm an overachiever by nature. When I approach something, I dedicate myself to it fully. I do that with every task. If it requires my time and effort, it's worth giving my full attention. Tackling two degrees at once allowed me to keep my focus where I felt it belonged.

WHY DO YOU WANT TO WORK FOR PRIMAL INSTINCTS?

Thinking: *I believe there's a secret sex club somehow tied to the company, and my main objective is to uncover it because, as I said, I'm inquisitive.*

Say: Because you're an industry leader. Unlike some gym chains that have focused on quantity, Primal Instincts focuses on quality. That's been seen by the steady increase in memberships across the country and the incorporation of other business lines over the years. But it's the all-inclusiveness that's the main draw. You're not solely focused on getting people in the door; it's about the science behind it. As a student of psychology, the idea of playing even a small role in that intrigues me.

WHY DO YOU BELIEVE YOU'RE THE BEST FIT FOR THE POSITION?

Thinking: *I'm a closet submissive, and I believe that uncovering the secret sex club might be the equivalent of discovering the fountain of youth. And it gives me something to do when I'm bored.*

Say: I'm the best person for the position because of my research, organization, and analytical skills. I hope to use these skills to launch successful rollouts of new products across all lines of business, utilizing the strength of the company's mission and the team environment as a springboard.

1

Journey

"AND THAT, MY FRIENDS, IS THE COMPLETION of your first-day orientation. Any questions?"

Oh, yeah. I had lots.

Is there a secret sex club hidden beneath this building? Are there secret exits? If so, how do you identify them? Will I recognize the members? Do they wear masks? Pins? Wristbands? Or do they have a special tattoo?

I didn't raise my hand since none of those questions pertained to anything I'd learned today and would likely get my fancy new security badge confiscated if they came tumbling out of my mouth.

Not to mention I was ready to be done with the whole orientation thing. I woke up that morning with a spring in my step, thinking I was about to start the first day of the rest of my life. More accurately, my new job at Primal Instincts, LLC, the company taking the country by storm with its innovation and dedication to health and wellness in all aspects of life.

Okay, fine, that was a direct quote from the LinkedIn job description I read back when I started searching for my way into this labyrinth of secrets disguised as a corporate giant. Even after listening to Nicholas Weston, a.k.a. Whiskey-Eyes, who was tasked with leading today's session, I hadn't yet bought into the hype. Not sure I ever would. And that wasn't me being skeptical. Well, maybe a little. While I applauded their efforts to change the world through exercise science, my motives for being there weren't exactly altruistic.

The good news, as Whiskey-Eyes had so kindly noted, the day was finally over.

Nick cleared his throat when no one raised their hand. "All right. I guess that'll conclu—"

No, no, no-o-o. Don't stop!

I could practically feel the dismissal slipping through my fingers as Nick stopped mid-sentence to peer toward the back of the room.

All heads turned, including mine, to see who was responsible for prolonging the torture.

Just inside the doorway, there was a perky brunette with an airplane-blinding shine on her lips to go with her self-tanner orange skin, smiling at someone outside the room. A second later, the mystery guest strolled through the doorway.

Oh boy.

I was pretty sure I wasn't the only one whose mouth went Mohave desert dry.

At the door, Pumpkin Barbie fluttered her fake lashes and flashed eerily white teeth at the man who looked her way and nodded, an expression of obvious appreciation on his face.

Do you appreciate her opening the door, big guy? Or has she done something else for you lately?

Yep, that was me being catty. I was single. He was hot. It was allowed.

A few seats down from me, a couple of people started whispering, but I couldn't make out what they were saying. My brain stopped performing like the well-educated machine that it was because it'd been overtaken by my hormones. That was what happened when an attractive man stepped into my visual range, and this man … he was quite possibly the most attractive man on the planet.

For a frame of reference, imagine what the offspring would look like if Michael Fassbender (no one rocks a tux better), the Mountain from *Game of Thrones* (because this guy was massive), Liev Schreiber from *Ray Donovan* (for that bad boy thing), and Ryan Reynolds (just because he's freaking gorgeous!) were to genetically mutate their sperm and have a child. *In case you're having trouble doing the mental manipulation, sinfully hot is what you'd get.*

"Creed," Nick greeted with a surprised grin.

"That's him," someone whispered excitedly. "That's Creed Granger."

This time their words processed at the same time my hypothalamus kicked into high gear as I drank in the sight of this ... this ... alpha male ... *god*.

If I had a *type*, at least from a physical perspective, Creed Granger would check all the boxes. Then again, when I arrived this morning, I might've said the same thing about Nick. In my defense, I found tall, muscular, well-dressed men attractive. Even better were the ones who invested in bespoke suits. That was my kryptonite. And fine, I didn't date much ... well, not *ever*, really, but that didn't mean I didn't have a keen eye.

To be fair, that keen eye had been locked on Creed Granger for longer than I cared to admit. I'd absorbed every detail I could uncover about him since, for all intents and purposes, this man was my mark. Yes, I said it like I was some super spy when in reality, I was more like Lucy Ricardo trying to find a jewel thief on a train bound for New York— an episode abound with antics and a bad guy she all but handed the jewels over to herself. Unfortunately, my efforts to get the dirty deets had failed as epically as Lucy's had.

At six feet, five inches, Creed Granger didn't only appear larger than life, he *was* larger than life. He was one of those people who had to duck when walking into a room to avoid bruising his forehead on the doorjamb. And the bespoke suit I mentioned before … well, Creed's was charcoal gray with pinstripes and custom-tailored to fit his large physique. There was no hiding the fact he was sporting some serious musculature beneath. Especially if the strong column of his neck was any indication.

His thick black hair was just a little too long—intentional, I figured—with a slight curl at the nape. His clean-shaven jaw looked like it'd been chiseled from granite, his cheekbones high and prominent. His nose … well, it wasn't perfect, but perhaps it could've been at some point in his life. Even though it appeared to have been broken at one time or another, it didn't detract from his devastatingly handsome face. In fact, it only drew attention to his eyes.

Oh, man, his eyes. Even from ten feet away, I could see the gloom of storm clouds in the quicksilver depths.

It was possible I was having a hot flash. And if I wasn't, I did the moment he spoke in that deep, dark baritone that was the equivalent of distant thunder, rhythmic and soothing as it rumbled across the sky.

"Since I'm not known for long-winded conversations," Creed began, "I have no intention of boring you any more than Nick has already." He flashed a crooked smile at Nick, then turned his attention back to the group. "I just wanted to introduce myself. I'm Creed Granger, the founder and CEO of Primal Instincts."

I heard the words coming out of his mouth, but he might as well have been speaking Klingon. The analytical side of my brain had taken a sabbatical, making it impossible for me to do anything more than fantasize about what dirty words might come from those full, perfect lips in the dark of night.

While I couldn't translate his language due to my libido being on the fritz, I *could* tell he was not new to public speaking because he was eloquent and controlled, engaging his audience with direct eye contact. He had that whole devil-may-care thing going on, suit jacket casually pulled back, hands tucked into his trouser pockets, and an expression that revealed his amusement plastered on his devastatingly gorgeous face.

I was tempted to look away when his gaze shifted to me, but at the last moment, I couldn't, and I found myself caught directly in the path of the tumultuous storm brewing in his eyes.

I knew it was my overactive imagination, but I swore something flashed hot in those gunmetal gray depths as they raked slowly over my face. My life hung in the balance for those too-brief moments when he gifted me with a smile before shifting his focus to the person on my right. I was still staring, which was why I noticed his gaze snapped back to mine almost instantly, and this time it wasn't my imagination. There was a twitch at the creased corners of his eyes—the barest hint of another smile, maybe?—that turned on the turbo boosters in my cardiovascular system.

Thankfully, he looked away, finishing his speech and allowing me to mentally crack the whip and wrangle in my lust. I'd never had that kind of physiological response to a man before, and I wasn't sure what to make of it.

Nick took over in that smooth, casual manner of his, offering a thank you to Creed for taking the time to come in before he officially released us for the evening.

I grabbed my purse and the leather-bound notebook I'd been jotting notes in all day, then set them both on the table in front of me and got to my feet. I dawdled a little longer than necessary, not wanting to risk having to walk out with Wayne Parson, one of the new hires who'd been hitting on me since I arrived at eight that morning. He was one of those pretty boys who bought his clothes directly out of the Bloomingdale's store window to prove he was hip to the current trend. You know, the kind who flashed a smile while he showed off his fake Patek Philippe watch because he thought women's panties fell right off from the gesture alone. I figured he was harmless and likely a natural flirt, but I lost my patience with him the third time he mentioned grabbing drinks after work. My initial decline should've been more than enough.

The good news was Wayne was long gone. The bad news … well, it looked like my plan to dodge Wayne backfired because now I was the only person left in the room besides Nick and Creed. Thankfully, they were whisper-deep in a conversation at the front, which meant there was still a chance I could make a clean getaway.

If I tip-toed.

Slowly.

Or not.

The moment I started toward the door, I saw Creed move out of the corner of my eye. He caught up to me when I was about a foot from freedom, pushing open the door to allow me to exit first.

"Thanks," I mumbled, peering up at him. My breath hitched when I met his gaze. From this distance, feet and inches seemed inconsequential in describing his enormous stature. An involuntary shiver rippled down my spine when our eyes locked. I'd never seen eyes that color before. Like steel in jewel form.

"Oh, hey, Journey! I think you left this," Nick called from inside the room.

"Interesting name," Creed said smoothly.

My best friend, Rhylee, would've referred to the rhythmic rumble as his Dom voice. You know, the kind that delivered words without inflection and commanded attention with a subtle drop in vocal range from tenor to baritone.

"I could say the same," I told him, flashing a smile and forcing myself to turn back to the room where Nick appeared in the doorway. "Thank you," I told him when he held out the notebook I'd left behind in my haste to get out of there.

"You're very welcome." Nick's hand brushed mine. "I'll see you around."

Will he? Or was that just something he said to all the new hires?

I flashed him a smile anyway, not sure what to say. When I turned back, I'd fully expected Creed to have left since I was sure he was a busy man, but no, he was still standing there, hands tucked in his pockets, suit jacket unbuttoned and pulled back as he leaned against the wall opposite the room. His gaze moved over me like that of a predator hunting his prey.

An enticing chill tickled my spine, but I shoved it aside, pretending not to notice. I looked left, then right, trying to remember which direction to go to reach the exit. The *real* exit, not the secret exit I had inadvertently looked for during one of our restroom breaks.

Creed offered assistance, standing tall and gesturing to my left before buttoning his jacket in that uber-hot way guys who wore suits did.

"I'll catch up with you in a bit," Nick told Creed before sauntering off in the opposite direction.

I couldn't resist watching him walk away because I'd been wondering whether or not Nick Weston looked as good from the back as he did from the front. For the record, he did. And I'd bet money he looked good naked, too.

Geez. What was *wrong* with me?

"What's your last name?"

I snapped my attention back to Creed, hoping he didn't see me ogling Nick's … *ass*ets. I was sure he did, but at least he had the decency not to call me on it. In my defense, it'd been a really long day.

"Zeplyn."

"Journey Zeplyn," he said as though wanting to feel the words on his tongue. That, or he was drawing the same conclusion most older people who met me did: I was named after the famous rock band. Perhaps two different bands.

And when I said older, I didn't mean Creed was an octogenarian. Based on my aforementioned research, he was thirty-nine, which was still young, but since he was fifteen when I was born, I got to categorize him as *older*.

Creed gestured for me to walk. "Your parents must love rock n' roll."

Yep, I had him pegged, alright.

I responded with the same thing I told everyone who looked at me like that when they heard my name. "They didn't *pick* the last name. Plus, Z-e-p-l-y-n. Not spelled the same."

"And the origination of *Journey*?"

My cheeks warmed from embarrassment because, yes, I was actually named after a famous rock band.

"You got me. My parents are sentimental romantics," I admitted. "'Faithfully' is their favorite song. But so is 'Crazy Train' by Ozzy. And no, before you ask, my middle name is not Ozzy." *But perhaps it should be Crazy Train after this conversation.*

His laugh was as deep and resonant as his voice, and another shiver ran over my skin at the sound.

"What *is* your middle name?"

"Don't have one. They couldn't choose between Aerosmith and Poison. Weird, right?"

He laughed again, and I swore I could feel the rumble deep inside me. Luckily, I didn't falter, keeping my stride loose yet purposeful as I made my way toward the main entrance.

"If I didn't know better, I'd think you were running away," Creed said casually, keeping pace with me.

"I only run if someone's chasing me with a knife."

Creed laughed, and I realized I'd said that out loud.

Warning! Your filter is malfunctioning. Pay attention.

"I'm heading home for the evening," I clarified, hating that the words didn't come out as confident as I had intended.

"I don't mind if you run." His tone was smooth and ridiculously sinful. "I like the chase."

Another chill slid through me, leaving goosebumps in its wake. Of all the men who might've shown interest, a self-made billionaire with a sketchy past was the absolute last person I should've found myself fascinated by. What could we possibly have in common?

Then again, did we need to have the same taste in music or books to enjoy spontaneous orgasms?

I mentally shook my head in disgust, completely disappointed that my hormones were wreaking serious havoc on my poor, overtaxed brain. Those were not the musings of a normal girl; they were that of a hussy who'd forgotten her reason for being here. Seriously, CEO … young, impressionable new hire … making small talk late in the day … deserted office building…

Sounded like a ridiculously common trope for a porn movie.

A little *too* cliché.

As I kept the exit in my sights, I reminded myself I wasn't here for orgasms, spontaneous or otherwise. Granted, I could only imagine a man who looked and sounded like Creed Granger would deliver one like no one else.

Enough with the orgasms!

My only goal was to uncover the dark underbelly hidden beneath this conglomerate. The secret world that existed only on the whispers of those who'd never so much as glimpsed the dark, seductive inner workings because those who *had* wouldn't dare reveal anything. According to rumors, sharing details was the one way to find yourself banned for life.

As I continued toward the exit, with Creed keeping pace, I reminded myself I had more important things to focus on than his Dom voice or his ridiculously big hands, or the sexy quirk of his dark eyebrows.

Long day, remember?

"Which department will you be working in?" he prompted, opening the door to the landing overlooking the lobby.

"Product marketing," I answered politely, grateful for the ability to focus on the steps beneath my feet rather than look up into that too-handsome face.

"For Cheryl?"

Assuming he was referring to Cheryl Mann, my new boss, I nodded. "That's my understanding."

"You'll like her."

I wanted to ask him why? Was she friendly? Funny? Lenient?

Thankfully, those questions remained firmly planted in my head.

When we reached the first floor, he was still with me, moving toward the main doors as I did. Again, he opened the door and stepped back, allowing me to walk through first. I was sure it was just a coincidence that we were going in the same direction, but it felt like more than that.

As soon as we stepped outside, I realized day was quickly giving way to night because that was what happened in February in Los Angeles.

Standing beneath the lit awning, I made a show of digging my car key out of my purse, expecting Creed to keep walking. He didn't, and when I found my key, I had no choice but to look up at him.

"It was nice to meet you," I managed, unable to hold that intense gray stare.

His smile was pure sin when he said, "Likewise."

I looked at the ground, at my key, at the parking lot that was quickly thinning out now that the workday had ended. Like a compass seeking north, my gaze lifted to his face one final time. "I … uh…" I motioned toward the parking lot and smiled. "I guess I'll go now."

Another smile pulled the corners of his mouth, making the skin around his eyes crinkle. "I look forward to seeing you around, Journey Zeplyn."

Really, it must be a company motto or something.

"Yeah." I nodded like an idiot. "You, too."

As I walked away, I prayed I didn't end up tripping over my own two feet and making a complete ass of myself.

2

Creed Granger

As I watched Journey walk away, I pulled out my cell phone, skimmed the contacts until I found the name I was looking for, then stabbed the phone to dial and pressed it to my ear.

A gruff voice answered with, "Ryder."

"Why the *fuck* didn't you tell me she was here?"

A short pause ensued, followed by, "Last I checked, I don't work for you, Granger."

Absolutely *not* the point.

"I should've been your first fucking phone call, and you know it," I hissed, hating that the gorgeous woman had blindsided me. To add insult to injury, she tripped my trigger *before* I realized who she was. Had someone given me a fucking heads-up, my damn dick wouldn't have been at risk of being choked by my goddamn zipper.

Journey fucking Zeplyn, the absolute last fucking woman on the face of the planet my cock had any business noticing.

"And what? You would've had the welcoming committee meet her at the door?" Ryder countered. "She woulda kicked my ass, and you know it."

"Next time I'm going to be blindsided by one of your offspring, I expect a goddamn call."

"She's my *only* offspring, asshole. And trust me, if I could've kept her away, you know I would've."

I suspected that was true, considering. "She still on her fact-finding mission?"

Ryder huffed. "More than ever. Damn girl doesn't know what's good for her."

I found it interesting that there was a wealth of adoration in the man's tone. Then again, Journey was likely the only person in the world, aside from her mother, Cadence, who could turn hardcore men like Ryder and Roman Zeplyn into marshmallows.

I watched Journey's small SUV back out of a parking space.

"I expect you to keep her from finding what she's looking for," Ryder said.

I didn't miss the underlying threat, nor did the double meaning escape me. Ryder had been warning me away from his daughter since I first saw her seven years ago when she was a fresh-faced seventeen-year-old about to graduate high school. I figured I was why they had encouraged her to go to Princeton rather than stay here in California and go to UCLA, which she'd had her heart set on. If she had been within my grasp, there was a damn good chance I would've ruined her by now. As it was, ruining her was the only thing I could think of when I looked at her.

"Please tell me you've got someone keeping an eye on her, Ryder."

"Not anymore."

"Why the fuck not?"

A hint of amusement sounded in his voice when Ryder said, "Because she gave me the high and mighty speech."

"I don't know what the fuck that means."

"Sure you do, Creed. You're a smart fucking man, and she's an independent woman who resents having her fathers hire someone to shadow her every move. It's not like I could tell her *why* we sicced a guard dog on her. Not without revealing the exact damn thing she's looking to unearth."

"Bullshit," I countered. "You're famous, Ryder. That's the only excuse you need."

"*Off-screen* famous," he corrected. "Not the same thing."

I knew Ryder, and I knew he would argue every point I made. Since it was all irrelevant at this point, I exhaled roughly.

"I figure she's safe with you around," Ryder said, clearly amused by my outburst.

I didn't hide the dark rumble of laughter. "Safe? You think your little girl is *safe* with me?"

He hesitated. "I know you'll look after her."

He was right about that. I would. Probably not the way a father wanted a man like me to look after his daughter, but sure, let's go with that.

"*Look* after," Ryder reiterated. "That doesn't mean touch, goddammit."

I recalled the moment our eyes met. I'd had to do a double take, but there hadn't been an ounce of recognition in her teal-blue eyes.

"She has no idea who I am?"

"You've never been introduced, so I'd say no." Ryder chuckled softly. "As I said … she's on a fact-finding mission."

"And she suspects my company is a front for a sex club?"

He laughed. "You say it like it isn't true."

"It's not true."

"Maybe not literally, but it does cover the cost of upkeep."

"Touché." I watched Journey's taillights disappear when she turned left out of the parking lot. "She's heading out now."

"Good. She survived the first day."

"I said it so you'd know to expect her."

"Two problems with that. One, we're not home. And two, she doesn't live with us."

"What?" I managed to bite my tongue to keep from demanding to know where he was.

"Do you really want me to repeat it?"

I exhaled sharply, debating whether I should skip my meeting and follow Journey home so that I could keep an eye on her.

"Creed, I know you think she's fragile, but she's not. My little girl's stronger than you give her credit for. She's her mother's daughter, and you, of all people, know what that means. So, I'll tell you the same thing we tell our overprotective wife: stand down and let her make her own way."

I huffed in exasperation. "When will you be back?"

"Two weeks. We left this morning. With Journey's blessing. She's staying at the house while we're gone. She's safe there."

"And you know this how?"

Ryder huffed a laugh. "Trust me, Creed. I know what I'm doing. The only thing you should be worried about going forward is my baby girl figuring out who you are. That, or stealing your job. Don't let protecting one cost you the other." Ryder laughed. "If you need anything, let us know."

I disconnected the call because nothing more needed to be said.

I was torn between following Journey home to ensure she got there safely and going about my regularly scheduled life. Although I had my doubts, I wanted to trust that Ryder and Roman knew what they were doing regarding Journey's safety. No way would they put their daughter in harm's way. Not if they could help it.

Before I could decide, my cell phone rang, and my assistant's name appeared on the screen.

"I'm heading out," I said when I answered.

"Your car is waiting for you when you're ready."

I hired Duke Mitchell to be my assistant for a reason. Well, a couple of them, actually. Mainly because he was efficient at doing precisely what I needed without question or hassle. Secondly, he knew who I was, and since he was a member of Primal—the secret club Journey was looking to unearth—he was sworn to secrecy. Living a double life wasn't as easy as it was cracked up to be, especially when the company I founded was rumored to be a cover for the world I'd built it on. I trusted Duke, which was not something I could say about many people in my life. Even after all these years, he'd proven to be the most valuable hire I'd made to date.

"I'm on my way around now," I told him. "I'll see you in the morning."

"Yes, sir."

I disconnected the call and tucked my phone in my pocket as I made my way to the executive building's main entrance. It was a nice evening, so I didn't mind the exercise. I wished it did more to clear the thoughts from my head, but it didn't.

Speaking of thoughts … they returned to the beautiful blonde who had disappeared into the night a short time ago.

Tucking my hands in my pockets, I glanced toward the parking lot. She was no longer there, but I could still see her in my mind. It was good that she had made a hasty exit; otherwise, I might've been inclined to disrupt my perfect record of never mixing it up with someone who worked for me.

And to think Ryder believed his daughter was safe in my presence. Like hell.

"Good evening, sir," my driver greeted as I approached the Cadillac Escalade waiting for me.

"Mason," I acknowledged.

He didn't have to ask where I wanted to go. He already knew.

I got in and focused my attention out the window.

Journey Zeplyn.

Her name was on repeat in my head for the five-minute drive from the office to Austere, the cigar bar where I was due for my standing Monday night meeting. It was a good thing I had a driver taking me to my destination because not only was her name rolling around in my gray matter, but her face seemed to be imprinted on my brain, her smile flashing in my mind's eye over and over again.

I couldn't stop thinking about her, although I didn't know why that was. I met beautiful women every single day. In this industry and this city, in particular, it wasn't uncommon to encounter good-looking people from all walks of life. From personal trainers to trophy wives to CrossFit addicts, when you were focused on giving people the tools necessary to improve their health, it was par for the course.

So it wasn't necessarily Journey's beauty—though she was striking—that I was captivated by. I wouldn't deny she had caught my attention when I saw her in that conference room, but that didn't explain the obsession I'd developed with her seven years ago. Granted, I should've questioned my sanity back when I first laid eyes on her.

As we neared our destination, that memory came to life in brilliant Technicolor detail.

"I'm glad you could make it," Ryder greeted from his post at the doors of the large ballroom.

"And you owe me twenty." Roman smirked at his twin. *"You said he wouldn't come."*

"How could I miss it?" I countered, shaking both of their hands. *"Your lovely wife only turns forty once."*

Ryder cocked an eyebrow. *"Don't let her hear you say that word."*

"She added it to the banned-in-the-house word list," Roman chimed in.

I glanced between them. "You have one of those?"

Ryder grinned. *"She knows better. But seriously, thanks for coming."*

Roman said, *"We know vanilla parties aren't your thing."*

"I make an exception for friends," I told them.

"Head to the bar," Ryder said. *"Say hello to the birthday girl on your way. Cadence is wandering around somewhere."*

I nodded at my friends before wandering the room. I took stock of who was in attendance, making note of those I recognized and those I didn't. Since it was a vanilla party, as Ryder had referred to it, there were a lot of people outside the scope of my world. Because of their profession, Ryder and Roman had garnered a lot of friends over the years. Many powerful, wealthy friends. Many people in this town would use the opportunity to introduce themself to the one person who could launch their career or skyrocket their stock. I wasn't like most people. I wasn't there to rub elbows with the rich and famous. I wasn't a name-dropper, so I didn't feel the need to get on anyone's radar. The path I paved in this world was my own. It didn't include stones of others tossed in along the way.

"Creed."

At the sound of my name, I turned to find Cadence Zeplyn smiling over at me. The elegant beauty didn't look a day over thirty. Unlike many guests in this room, her good looks couldn't be attributed to a scalpel and a skilled surgeon.

"There's the birthday girl," I greeted, kissing both of her cheeks while she fought the urge to lower her eyes in submission. Cadence was a natural submissive—a masochist, if we were being specific—and though her vanilla persona directly contradicted her inner desires, she couldn't fight the urge when it arose.

"Thank you for coming."

I turned to face the room as she stood beside me. "Nice turnout."

"Between you and me, I requested a different venue."

I grinned down at her. "I'm sure that's next on their agenda. You know you're always welcome at the club."

"It's the only thing I had on my wish list. It's been too long." Cadence exhaled heavily.

"Aren't spankings a foregone conclusion on birthdays? You don't need a club for that."

Her cheeks turned a pretty rose, and this time she did avert her gaze even as she smiled. "One can hope."

"If you'd like, I'll be glad to drop a hint."

"Nothing too subtle. Perhaps a two-by-four upside the head." She laughed softly. "Sometimes I think they purposely forget our roots."

"I'll gladly do your bidding, my lady," I said dramatically, earning another laugh.

"*I would appreciate it. Anyway. I've got to mingle. My husbands don't like when I disappear for too long.*"

"*Enjoy.*"

While she went off to be the center of attention, I moved to the bar, took a seat, and got comfortable. I'd only come to make an appearance, and at the first opportunity, I intended to be out the door and off to the different venue Cadence had mentioned earlier. I could only handle so much vanilla in one night.

"*Scotch, neat,*" *I said when the bartender approached.*

He nodded in acknowledgment, then went to pour my drink. I glanced at the sea of faces, continuing to catalog who was who, skipping over those I'd never met.

"*Here you are, sir.*"

"*Thanks,*" *I told the bartender. I took a sip, scanned the room, and before the liquor could make it down my throat, she appeared.*

In that fleeting moment, everyone else in the room disappeared. Only the angel in white remained.

As with most haute couture, the dress she wore was hideous on a good day. Yet somehow, she made the white minidress with gaudy floral appliqués look sophisticated. The mock turtleneck didn't detract from her sleek neck, only drew attention to it, as did the way she wore her golden hair pinned high on her head in some complicated design. With her hair up, I had an unobstructed view of the smooth skin of her back, revealed by the numerous cutouts on the dress.

Even wearing five-inch razor-thin stilettos, she moved across the room with purpose and grace. There was no doubt she embraced who she was, but it was the elegance in the way she walked, the sweet smile that curved her glossy pink lips when she greeted those who stopped her that captivated me. At one point, she glanced in my direction, and I got a glimpse of teal-blue eyes, the color so vibrant, it didn't look real.

I couldn't look away, even when a woman approached me, trying to make conversation. I ignored her, absorbing every inch of the flaxen-haired beauty as she slowly made her way across the room, moving away from me. It wasn't until she approached Cadence that I saw the resemblance. It was in their smile and the shape of their eyes, the silky gold of their hair.

Yep, it was just my luck that the woman who'd bewitched me in a way no other ever had was none other than Journey Zeplyn. Ryder, Roman, and Cadence's seventeen-year-old daughter.

That night had been etched into my brain for seven long years. I'd never forgotten Journey Zeplyn's effect on me. I'd felt something eerily similar when I saw her in the conference room. I'd been skimming faces, not giving them time to register, delivering my speech as I did at every new hire orientation because Nick insisted it softened my image. But the instant I saw those blue eyes, I had to do a double-take to confirm the déjà vu I felt.

Needless to say, the impact she had on me today was the same as it had been that night. Everyone else faded until we were the only two people in the room. For whatever reason, seeing her triggered something inside me. Something even darker than I thought existed.

It was just a damn good thing I was proficient at my job. I didn't miss a beat, welcoming the newest members of the Primal Instincts team even as I mentally calculated her age to ensure my thoughts weren't illegal.

A better man would've pretended not to see her. At the very least, I should've shoved her into the back of my mind the way I had for the past seven years. I had no business thinking about her or anticipating all the wicked, filthy things I wanted to do to her luscious body. Journey Zeplyn was the last woman on earth I should want, and for more reasons than merely the fact I was friends with her parents. At the top of that list: the things I wanted and expected from a woman weren't what she was equipped to give me. Journey couldn't possibly understand the darkness that lurked in a man, the desires he was plagued with when he accepted that he engaged his primal side. The lifestyle I lived was based on that ingrained instinct, the one that the alpha of every pack was born with: a need to dominate.

Perhaps because of those dark desires, I'd never been attracted to petite women. It made no fucking sense that part of Journey's appeal was that very trait. Her diminutive stature spoke to me on a baser level. I figured she was about five feet tall, but she probably told everyone she was five-two. Since I was six-five, there'd be some definite challenges, but I was sure we could overcome them.

Yes, that was me fantasizing when I had no business doing so.

The thought of a tiny thing breaking because I was too big or too rough didn't appeal. And everything about her was small, from her cute nose to her delicate fingers. Beneath her blue cashmere sweater, I could tell her breasts were equally proportionate to the rest of her. Not that I minded. I liked tits as much as the next guy, but I was more of an ass man, and hers... Jesus. I'd been mesmerized when she was walking toward her car, the charcoal gray slacks she wore encasing what might be perfection.

I sighed. I was a man of principles, and seven years ago, only a few weeks shy of her eighteenth birthday, she'd been far too young for the likes of me. Even now, I should likely take into consideration the difference in our ages. Having recently turned thirty-nine, I wasn't looking to relocate to a nursing home anytime soon, but I was no spring chicken either. With a fifteen-year age gap, it was difficult not to wonder whether we'd have anything in common. Yet I still fantasized about her sitting astride my cock and riding me like a Harley.

But the truth was, Journey Zeplyn was no longer an impressionable young girl. Her beauty had matured the same as her age, and she was even more sinfully irresistible than she had been back then. The instant I saw the long fall of board-straight silk that cascaded down her back, I wondered what it would feel like sliding through my fingers, how cool it would be against my naked chest while she hovered over me, riding my dick.

And her eyes. The color drew you in and held you there against your better judgment. A potent swirl of cool aqua blue and deep teal green. They glittered when she smiled as though backlit by a light from within.

But the one thing about her that struck a chord inside me was her voice. I hadn't had the pleasure of hearing it seven years ago, and it was probably a good thing. It wasn't what you expected from such a little thing like her—a tad husky, a lot raspy ... an audible seduction with every single syllable. I could still hear it and vividly recalled how my body reacted to the first words she spoke.

To complicate matters further, she worked for me, and I'd made it this far in life by keeping my professional and personal lives separate. Completely. It wasn't an option because I lived by a code: protect what was most important. I pushed limits on a daily basis, took risks others claimed were foolhardy, and craved things most deemed inappropriate. So when it came to my personal endeavors, I made a point to tread lightly. I figured that was the only explanation for how much I'd accomplished in my life and how I'd lived this long.

Any rational man would take that list of cons and toss the idea in the discard pile. When weighed against the pros, at least at this phase, it didn't make sense.

However, because of my natural inclination to go against the norms of society, I wasn't ready to do that just yet. The moment I saw her all those years ago, something inside me had come alive. And it'd been dormant until today. The moment I realized who she was, it was as though a switch had been flipped and a path to a new adventure had been revealed.

No, it wasn't like me to wax poetic, but here I was.

Thankfully, I arrived at my destination, and I knew for the next couple of hours at least, Journey Zeplyn would no longer be a distraction.

We'd call that wishful thinking.

3

Journey

"TELL ME, TELL ME, TELL ME!" RHYLEE squealed in my ear.

"Tell you what?" I said, pretending it was just an ordinary day, not the first day of a new adventure.

"Seriously? You never bothered to tell me you *got* the job until you *started* the job, and you're gonna act like you don't know what I'm talking about?"

She was right that I didn't tell her. The last time I talked to Rhylee, she said she was suffocating beneath the weight of her latest literary masterpiece—she wrote erotic romance, and yes, as far as I was concerned, it was literary gold—so she had politely excused herself to deal with her muses.

And because, at that point, it had been nearly a month and a half since I first applied for the job, I figured it was easier to keep the details to myself until there was something to talk about. As it was, the hiring process had been ridiculous. Between the tedious interactions with the recruiter, the holidays sneaking in, and the entire month of January, which apparently disrupted the company because it was their busiest time of the year, plus the rigorous interview process, it had taken more than sixty days from start to finish.

Start being my application and *finish* being the interview, which occurred *three weeks* ago.

They had called and officially offered me the position *two weeks* ago. On a Friday. January twentieth, to be exact. A little after three in the afternoon.

I knew because I hyperventilated a little as soon as I saw the company name on the screen. I remembered thinking that whoever was on the other end of that phone was about to make me have a crappy weekend or a really good one. Reluctantly, I answered and got the thrilling news and the promise of an official offer letter via email. I pretty much accepted without seeing the pay and spent the weekend wishing I could celebrate with Rhylee. Instead, my parents took me to dinner at CUT, my absolute favorite place to eat.

"You owe me a hundred bucks, by the way," I told Rhylee. "I told you I could do it."

"How about I pick up the tab for dinner next time we go out?"

"Deal."

"That's settled, so tell me everything."

"Well, I spent eight solid hours sitting in a hard plastic chair with a room full of people while we listened to the monotonous drone of policy and procedure dubbed new-hire orientation by some sadist with too much time on his hands. The only exciting part was when I didn't know whether I'd ever get feeling in my left butt cheek again."

"Liar," she giggled. "If you don't tell me right this minute, I'm coming over, and I'll beat on your door until you answer."

"Your knuckles will bleed 'cause I'm not home."

"Oh, shit. That's right. You're at your folks' house."

"Cat-sitting," I clarified.

I had seen through my parents' request for me to cat-sit a long time ago. After all, they employed people who could look in on the cats or even stay here if they preferred. But since they felt more comfortable with me staying at their house, I pretended not to know that they were using it as an excuse. Since they lived in a gated community with twenty-four-hour on-site security *and* they had a security gate at the entrance to the house, it was pretty much a fortress, so I understood their reasons.

"You're drinking wine, aren't you?" Rhylee asked.

"I am. Second glass." I relaxed back on the butter-soft leather sofa, my feet up on the ottoman, one cat staring at me while another did a tightrope walk across the narrow ledge behind me.

"Are you tipsy yet?"

"Probably. Your point?"

"When you're tipsy, you never shut up. So spill."

"What do you wanna know?"

"Who did you meet?"

I sighed. "It was orientation. Mostly new people."

"Who led it?"

I paused for dramatic effect. "Nicholas Weston."

"Oh."

"Oh?" I prompted. "What's that mean? *Oh* good? Or *oh* bad?"

"Just *oh*," she clarified. "What's he like?"

"Nice," I said, knowing that wasn't what she wanted to know. "Very eloquent. He's a good teacher."

Rhylee snorted. "He's hot, right?"

"So hot."

"Describe him."

I took a sip of wine. "I'd say he's close to six feet, lean, muscular. Nice dresser."

"Suit?"

"Yep. Navy-blue." She didn't stop me, so I rambled on. "Dirty blond hair, whiskey gold eyes. Quick to smile and laugh. He got a lot of calls, and when he checked his phone, he seemed pissed."

I didn't tack on that I assumed his ex-wife was blowing up his phone. Considering his divorce made *Page Six* headlines when his now ex-wife accused him of being aggressive and dominating in the bedroom, I didn't think it was a stretch. Of course, he denied the accusations but refused to comment to quash the attention. It worked. Mostly.

"Who else did you meet?"

I knew there was only one person Rhylee cared about. That was how it'd been since I first told her my suspicions about a secret fetish club a couple of months after we met. Being that she wrote BDSM romance novels, I figured she would get a kick out of it. She'd been intrigued when I mentioned the Dominant they referred to only as Alpha. As for who he was, I had no idea. Everything I'd ascertained was a myth because no one who was a member would ever divulge the secret. She didn't seem to care because ever since I told her the CEO of Primal Instincts, LLC, fit the profile of the ultimate Dominant, she'd had her submissive heart set on him.

"You're killing me, Journey. Tell me!"

I giggled, then let his name fall from my lips reverently. "Creed Granger."

"What?"

"Creed. Granger," I repeated slowly.

"I know what you said. You *met* him?"

"Yeah."

"The CEO?"

"One and the same."

"The man you believe is the ultimate Dominant?"

"I never said that," I corrected. "I said he fits the profile based on what I've read about him."

"The question is, does he *look* the part?"

"You've seen pictures. What do you think?"

"Pictures don't do most people justice."

She was right. And they certainly didn't do Creed justice. "So?"

I giggled. "Yeah, he looks the part."

Rhylee sighed.

I did *not* tell her that I walked out of the building with him or that I'd had numerous fantasies about stripping off that immaculate suit piece by piece so I could discover how many licks it would take to get to the center of an uber-hot CEO.

"What's he like?"

"I don't even know what that means. Do you want to know the color of his eyes or whether he has bad breath? I don't know what he's like. Tall. Like seriously tall."

"You're five foot nothing. Everyone's tall to you."

"That's fair. Plus, he was only in there for like two minutes."

"Describe him."

"Tall," I repeated simply to irk her. "He had to duck to get through the door. Black hair, gray eyes, clean-shaven." I was trying to sound as though I wasn't at all intrigued. "He's a suit guy. Rocks the *shit* out of a suit."

"What else did you find out about him?"

"It wasn't a speed dating session. I didn't get to ask him questions."

"Should I be worried that you know what speed dating is?"

"I'm a worldly woman. You don't know how I spend my three- to six-minute increments. I might be well-versed in rapid-fire terminology."

Rhylee laughed.

"But if you're thinking I found the signs pointing me toward the secret entrance to the secret club, they weren't hanging on the wall. The exit signs are really exit signs. I didn't see any secret handshakes, either."

"You're a pain in the ass; you know that?"

"So I've been told. How's the book coming along?" I asked because I honestly didn't have much to tell her. I knew going into this that it would take time and patience before I might get a single clue (if the club existed), and though I'd told her as much, she was the type who wanted things yesterday.

"It stalled," she said, sounding crestfallen.

"What? Really? I thought they were banging like rabbits. Upside down, was it? Tied to a flagpole? I can't remember. Maybe it was a telephone pole."

"You're funny." She sighed again. "My muse just dried right on up."

I took a sip of wine and grinned. "Like vaginal dryness? That's not good in romance novels, is it?"

She snorted. "Girl, you kill me. So what do you plan to look for tomorrow?"

I should've known she wasn't ready to move on. "I figure the first few weeks will be me trying to ramp up. It *is* a real job. I'm sure I'll have tasks to complete."

"I want you to find out more about the CEO."

"I doubt he'll be lured into revealing incriminating details over lunch, Rhylee."

"You won't know unless you try. And if anyone can do it, it's you."

I seriously doubted that. A fishing expedition to uncover a secret kink club probably needed better bait than a twenty-four-year-old almost virgin. And by *almost*, I meant I'd had sex with exactly one man … or rather, boy, in my life. We were seventeen at the time, and it was a lackluster event, to say the least. He took my virginity on the sofa in the game room of his parents' house while we were watching TV. He spent so much time feeling me up that he had nothing left for the encore, and after his two-minute race to the finish line, he left me wondering why in the world I'd given my V-card to him in the first place.

"I'll do my best," I promised.

"Call me tomorrow and let me know how day two goes."

"I will. And in the meantime, get your muse gal some K-Y. I hear it works wonders."

"My muse is a guy."

"Oh. In that case … I'm not sure about lubricant, but I know they make a delay spray for dudes. He'll last a loooooong time."

The last thing I heard was Rhylee's snort as I ended the call.

4

Creed

As I ALWAYS DID WHEN I AUSTERE, I greeted those I recognized, both staff and customers. I'd owned the bar for eight years, and until recently, I'd spent a good amount of my time there. It was previously a nightclub, but I'd converted it into a restaurant/cigar lounge when I purchased it. I had two reasons for doing so, the first being I was too fucking old for nightclubs. And secondly, by turning it into a place I enjoyed going, I shared similar interests with most of my clientele.

Some believed that Primal Instincts, LLC, was a cover for my true passion, Primal, the clandestine, members-only BDSM club I oversaw. They were wrong. But Austere was very close to being one. However, I would consider it more of a bridge between the two worlds, not exactly a cover. It wasn't that I needed another form of income to cover my extracurricular activities. Still, when I decided to open Austere, I'd been looking for something that would allow the members of Primal to interact in a vanilla setting if they were so inclined.

To most people, Primal was merely a myth, but to our 264 members, it was very real. By design, nothing would tie either of my companies to the club, although I wasn't above leaking rumors to redirect when I thought someone was getting too close to figuring out the truth. The most recent rumor was that a labyrinth of secret passageways and playrooms connected the two buildings. There weren't any, but that hadn't stopped several people from trying to find out for themselves.

Austere was the exact opposite of its name. Rather than severe or strict, it was an upscale, highly luxurious cigar lounge that catered to those who preferred and could afford the finer things in life. We were open to the public from two in the afternoon to two in the morning, with dinner service seven days a week. There were two bars, two lounges, the restaurant dining area, plus a private room we rented for special occasions. On a good night, we were at capacity by nine, with dinner reservations booked out a month in advance. And on the weekend, the line to get into the lounge was two blocks long.

"We're not to be bothered," I told the hostess as I made my way to the private room.

She offered a pleasant smile, then closed the door when I walked inside.

Within a minute of my arrival, a glass of Macallan Rare Cask was placed in front of me. I didn't have to state my brand preference or that I wanted my whiskey neat; they knew what I liked. A moment later, my personal humidor and Zippo lighter were set on the large round table, and three crystal ashtrays were delivered. Within two minutes, I was no longer alone. Two of my best friends/business partners arrived, taking their seats. More drinks were delivered, and the humidor was passed around while we waited for the fourth arrival.

Aside from Primal, Austere was the one place we regularly frequented because it was a protected space. Jammers were installed in this room and the VIP lounge, which kept prying ears from overhearing anything we said. It might seem like overkill, but in a city overrun by people who wanted to get paid for the next TMZ headline, it was necessary. We were waited on only by members of Primal, who were sworn to secrecy thanks to an iron-clad non-disclosure agreement. Simply put, we didn't have to worry about what we said or did within these four walls.

"Did Duke talk to you about my proposal for the charity function?"

Not that we talked about anything but work.

"You mean your annual decades party," I clarified. "What decade is it this year?"

"The eighties."

"You realize most of our employees weren't even alive in the eighties."

"All the better," Nick said with an eye roll. "The point of the original question was the proposal."

The whiskey went down smoothly as I pondered my response. "If he deems it important, he'll ensure I see it."

Nick rolled his eyes again. He was like a five-year-old that way. "That's a yes, then."

I smiled as I set my glass down and picked up the cigar cutter. Sometimes Nick asked the most asinine questions. He should've known by now that anything he sent got passed directly to me. He didn't give himself enough credit, though. Hence the stupid question.

"We're not seriously gonna talk about work, are we?"

The question came from Jacob Hawkins, known only as Hawk to anyone who interacted with him personally and plenty who didn't.

"Why wouldn't we?" I countered, making a small cut on the cigar cap and passing the cutter to him.

One arched eyebrow slid up toward his hairline. "Seriously? Did you not get a look at the new hires?"

Because the mere mention of new hires made me think of golden hair and otherworldly blue eyes, I grabbed my drink, tossing back what was left in it.

"What does that have to do with anything?" I asked, setting the empty glass down. "And how'd *you* get a look at them?"

Hawk jerked his chin toward Nick, who was sitting opposite me, a shit-eating grin on his smug face.

I sighed and gave in to my curiosity. "Who's on your radar this time?"

"Jesus, man. Don't tell me you didn't see her," Hawk said, staring at the glowing end of his cigar as he tilted his glass toward his lips.

There was movement at my side as my empty glass was removed, a fresh one placed in its spot.

"Who?" I asked, feeling a hint of trepidation forming in my gut.

"Oh, he saw her all right," Nick told Hawk, his eyes glittering even in the dimly lit space. "He walked her to her car."

I should've known.

I glanced between Nick and Hawk, frowning. "Journey?"

"Oh, fuck." Hawk set his cigar in the giant crystal ashtray so he could put his hand over his heart. "That's her name? She's an angel, man. I'm gonna marry that girl." He mumbled her name before taking a swig from his glass.

I didn't mention her last name because as soon as I did, Hawk would want to eat those words.

"Good luck," Nick told Hawk. "You might have to fight Wayne for her hand in marriage."

"Who the fuck's Wayne?" Hawk asked, a menacing snarl on his lips.

"Some fucker who can't take a hint." Nick laughed. "Guy hit on her all damn day, even when she turned him down for drinks. Three fucking times."

"So you're saying she's available." Hawk's grin returned as he picked up his cigar. "I call dibs."

I should've expected that. Unlike me, the man had a thing for blondes—especially petite ones. Then again, Hawk had a penchant for pretty much all women. And some men.

I looked at Nick. "Please tell me you didn't drag Garrison over to see her."

"He most certainly did," Garrison called from behind me as he approached the table. "Sorry, I'm late. Meetin' ran long. What'd I miss?"

With drink in hand, Garrison Walker, the VP of Product Management and one of my best friends for the past two decades pulled out the fourth chair and dropped into it, his gaze skimming each of us in turn as he settled in for the long hall.

"Journey, the angel," Hawk crooned.

Garrison's eyebrows dipped down. I could tell he was trying to pretend he didn't notice her, but I could see through him. "Who's that?"

"The blonde from the new hire class," Nick offered. "Big blue eyes."

"Ah, hell." A grin split Garrison's face. "She's somethin', huh?"

Somethin' wasn't quite the right word for what she was, but I didn't tell them that. I did, however, settle back in my chair and puff on my cigar, steadily observing my best friends.

Jacob "Hawk" Hawkins was the youngest at thirty. In some ways, he hadn't changed much since his early twenties when I met him at the height of his UFC career, long before I convinced him to become the face of Primal Instincts, LLC. He had never been married, never even been in a serious relationship—the kind with the potential for a future, at least—and he had no intention of being in one. Hawk believed that if God intended for a man to settle down with one woman, he wouldn't have made the next one hotter than the last.

Then there was Garrison Walker. He was thirty-nine—
ten months older than me—with an outlook on the world
very similar to mine. Garrison played the role of consummate
professional by day, but he reverted to the laidback country
boy we knew him to be the minute he walked out of the office.
He wasn't married, but he'd come damn close with one
woman roughly five years ago. Luckily for Garrison, the
woman propositioned Nick before they ever made it to the
church. Being a good friend, Nick shared the incident with
Garrison, giving him ample time to send her packing. He
hadn't dated anyone since, and as far as I knew, Garrison was
content with how things were going. Although complicated
was a good word to describe the situation he'd found himself
in, but that was a topic for another time.

To his left was Nicholas Weston. I'd known Nick a little
longer than I'd known Garrison. At thirty-six, he was recently
divorced. He was the only one of us who had ever taken the
plunge. We liked to give him shit, not because he took the
leap but because he chose a vanilla woman to put a ring on.
According to him, love made a man do strange things. As I
predicted, it didn't work out. When you were programmed a
certain way, it was damn near impossible to go against your
baser instincts. Unfortunately, Nick learned that the hard
way.

As for the four of us finding interest in the same woman
… I couldn't say it surprised me. I was more surprised that
it'd never happened before. Didn't matter that there were
plenty of women within arm's reach who wouldn't mind
spending a few hours in their company. They were going to
hone in on one for two reasons: first off, it was a challenge,
and second, it kept them entertained.

Since it was Hawk's mission in life to show us all up, there'd be no exception with Journey. He was going to ask her out. Probably first thing in the morning since the guy had no shame. Or patience. If she took him up on the offer of dinner—which she likely would since women tended to gravitate toward that bad boy charm—they'd have a good time. He'd wine and dine her for a few days, but the novelty would fade for him within that time frame because that darker instinct still drove him, and he could only pretend for so long. By then, Journey would be ready to move on because Hawk had the attention span of a squirrel.

The second Hawk looked away, Garrison was going to move in. Hawk would still technically be dating Journey when that happened. Garrison would use his love of music to get in good with a woman named after an iconic rock band. He'd make nice and befriend her first before he went in for the kill when she was hot and bothered because Hawk was no longer answering her calls. She'd be drawn to the country boy charm because women were, but more than likely, she'd relegate him to the friend zone because that seemed to be his preference.

And Nick … well, he'd play it safe and keep his distance. While Nick could flirt with the best of them, his rule was to take things slow, and these days, that translated to nowhere at all. As in, the last three vanilla women he'd gone out with since his divorce, he didn't sleep with until they'd hit their one-month mark. He would deny it, but I was sure the snail's pace routine was his excuse to keep the nightmare alive.

That was the way they operated, these friends of mine.

But what was wrong with the picture was that these men, with the exception of Nick, tended to keep their distance from vanilla women. Their desires ran too dark to risk it. More importantly, if I told them I was interested, they would back off. It was the natural order of things, and since Journey was the only woman who'd captured my attention in what felt like forever, they'd toe the line. Well, everyone except Hawk. He was a rebel, and no matter how hard I tried, I couldn't tame him.

"Creed?"

I glanced at Hawk to see that he was regarding me coolly. I figured he'd picked up on my inner turmoil because that was what he did. Because of our sordid history, Jacob Hawkins was primed to read me on a deeper level.

Hawk cleared his throat, his smile faltering. "What's going on?"

I took a sip of my drink, looked between them, and considered how I wanted to proceed.

"What aren't you tellin' us?" Garrison prompted.

I glanced at each of them. "Journey's last name is Zeplyn."

"As in Ryder and Roman's daughter?" Hawk asked, his surprise etched on every inch of his handsome, battle-scarred face.

"Oh, shit." Garrison's eyebrows slammed down as he glared at Nick. "Why the hell did you have us come look at her?"

Nick smirked. He was devious like that.

Hawk voiced the question I knew they were all thinking. "Is she off limits?"

I'd always known that one day I would meet the woman who would connect with the primal beast inside me. I'd anticipated it, even. But I never expected she would be so ill-equipped to handle what I'd want from her. Still, I wanted her.

"Creed?" Nick's tone was dark. "Lay it out clearly. Is Journey off limits?"

"Yes," I told them firmly.

Nick swallowed hard and reached for his glass, tossing it back.

"You protectin' her because she's their daughter? Or are you stakin' your claim?" Garrison asked, never one to give up on getting to the heart of the matter.

I met his gaze as the two options churned in my brain.

I peered at the lit end of my cigar. "The latter."

No one said a word. Whether it was because they were too stunned to speak or disappointed that they'd lost their chance with her was anyone's guess.

5

Journey

"GOOD MORNING, LOVELIES! NEW DAY, NEW LIVES to inspire. Don't get comfortable."

As I stood in the center of the space I was directed to when I arrived this morning, I found the source of the voice and gave my full attention to Cheryl Mann, my new boss. She was an older woman, mid- to late-fifties, I would guess. As she had been the day I met her in the interview, she was dressed professionally in a pair of light-gray slacks with a black silk blouse tucked into them. She was wearing a lightweight gray jacket that matched the pants. Her hair was a similar shade of gray, cut in a sleek, short bob that angled around her pretty face.

"Don't tell me we're moving again," someone grumbled.

A tall, stout redhead appeared, wearing a glower to go with formfitting khaki pants cropped just above the ankle, a black V-neck sweater, comfortable loafers, and no socks. Because of the androgyny of their appearance, I preferred not to assume they were male or female, something my mother taught me at a young age. Like Cheryl, their hair was short, not quite reaching their shoulders, the wavy red-gold strands loose around their face. They were pretty with a masculine edge. Probably had something to do with the fact they had more muscle than most of the men I knew.

"Yes, Gem, we are moving again." Cheryl's voice was chipper, her eyes kind as she regarded us. "And I'm thrilled to say it's for the last time. Where's Delaney?"

"I'm here!" a soft feminine voice sounded behind me. A moment later, a gorgeous, dark-skinned black woman appeared. Her head was a poof of silky curls, her lips a soft glossy pink, her eyes were the color of dark chocolate and enhanced by carefully applied makeup, and her smile was wide enough to flash pearly whites. She was tall, probably close to six feet in her chunky heeled boots. Her tan pants were loose-fitting, flaring around her feet, and her long-sleeve, purple shirt hugged her generous curves. She had a cross-body bag slung across her back, but as we stood there, she slipped it over her head and set it on the floor.

"There should be a fourth," Cheryl noted, peering around. When she didn't find who she was looking for, she turned back to us. "Well, hopefully, he'll show up sooner than later." She smiled. "Journey Zeplyn, I'd like you to meet your co-workers, Delaney Hill and Gemma Rosen."

Delaney's smile was friendly and kind as she stepped forward and held out a hand, her long fingers adorned with silver and gold.

I shook it. "Nice to meet you."

"Likewise." Her gaze swung to Cheryl. "If you'd've given us a heads up we had new people starting, I would've laced the brownies I made."

Cheryl laughed, shaking her head as she looked at me. "Ignore her. She speaks only to get a rise out of me."

Gemma wasn't quite so friendly, offering a nod in my direction. "I prefer Gem. And my pronouns are they/them."

They regarded me carefully as though anticipating a negative response. I could tell them that my mother was a clinical psychiatrist who specialized in gender and sexuality and that she raised me to understand that gender identity didn't always align with what was assigned at birth, but I figured the how and why weren't important.

"It's nice to meet you, Gem," I said politely. "I use she/her."

"Me, too!" Delaney chimed in gleefully. "I always forget to add that."

"She/her for me as well," Cheryl added.

Gem turned their attention back to Cheryl. "Where are we moving this time?"

"Our new floor is finally finished," Cheryl declared, looking pleased by the notion. "It's in the executive building. Sixth floor."

"Six?" Delaney squealed. "As in underneath seven?"

"And above five." Cheryl grinned. "That's correct, Delaney. You can go to the head of the class."

I wanted to ask what was special about the seventh floor, but I refrained.

"Finally," Gem grumbled. "We've been waiting a year for that shit to be done."

"It's only been six months," Cheryl corrected.

"Feels like a year."

"As does this conversation," Delaney noted with a huff of laughter. "What now?"

"You know the drill. Pack your things in the boxes I've placed on your desks and label them with your name. The movers will be coming through in"—Cheryl glanced at her watch—"thirty minutes."

And just like that, I was standing alone in the center of a row of cubicles while they scurried off to do their thing.

"Can I help anyone?" I offered.

"Oh, girl," Delaney chirped, her head appearing over the top of one wall. "I won't say no to help."

"That's because you need all the help you can get," Gem called back.

Delaney laughed. "I love your sense of humor, Gem. Glad to see you found it after all these years."

Grateful for something to do, I hurried toward Delaney's cube, set my bag on the hardback guest chair near the entrance, and headed to the opposite side of the eight-by-eight space.

"Just toss anything in the drawer right into the box. I'll sort it out when we get there."

I followed her instructions, transferring everything from the three wide drawers into one box, pretending not to be interested in all the pens, pencils, and knickknacks she had on hand.

"This is the third time we've moved since I started six months ago," Delaney explained. "They've been promising we'll have a permanent home eventually, but I was beginning to think we were being punked."

"Is the executive building far from here?" I asked.

"Technically, it's the same building, on the opposite end. You can only access it from the main lobby. It's a secured section."

I recalled having to badge into the building, then show that same badge to the man standing at the security desk. I wasn't sure how much more secure an area could be.

Could it be because they're hiding secret passageways?

"Because the executives are there?" I asked.

"That and product development," she replied, dumping a stack of thick notebooks into one of the boxes. "Intellectual property is a big deal, so they keep it secured." She motioned outside of the cubicle. "Ours is a relatively new team, so they've been trying to find a place where we fit."

"Who handled product launches before?"

"The marketing team. Since the product line keeps growing, they decided to expand with a specialized team."

Made sense.

I double-checked that all the drawers in the desk were empty, then grabbed one of the stickers from a roll sitting on the desk. I placed it on the top of the box, ready for Delaney to write her information, then stepped out into the aisle so I didn't crowd her while she finished.

"All done!" Delaney announced, her bag slung across her once more as she joined me. "Need help in there, Gem?"

"Do I *ever* need help?" The snide remark was muted through the wall.

"Don't let their grouchiness fool you," Delaney said with a laugh. "Underneath that rough exterior, Gem's just a sweet, little ol' teddy bear."

"I heard that," Gem called back, only this time, there was a hint of a smile in their tone.

A cell phone rang, then Cheryl's voice sounded from her office. "Thanks, Kurt. I'll swing by on our way to the executive building. Probably be ten minutes. Tell him to wait."

Gem stepped out of their cubicle, joining us. They were weighed down with a large leather briefcase dangling from one shoulder, an even bigger bag on the other, a rectangular insulated lunch box in one hand, and their cell phone clutched in the other.

"When are you gonna realize if it doesn't fit in one bag, you don't need it?" Delaney teased, motioning with a circle of her finger at Gem. "All that stuff's old-school."

"What you're trying to say is I'm old," Gem countered with a gleam of amusement in their eyes.

"Not old. Vintage," Delaney clarified.

Gem laughed, rolling their eyes. "I'm thirty-four. That doesn't quite qualify as vintage."

Delaney giggled. "To me, it does. I'm just a youngster." Her dark brown eyes shifted to me. "Or I thought I was before they started hiring babies. How old are you, Journey Zeplyn?"

There was no condescension in her tone, only a hint of a tease, so I deadpanned, "Thirty-eight." I touched my cheeks. "I've had a little work done. Pretty good, huh?"

Delaney's eyes went dinner plate wide. "Nuh-uh."

Gem snorted a laugh, their shoulders relaxing, although that heavy load still weighed them down.

I laughed. "Twenty-four."

"Girl, I was about to ask for the number of your plastic surgeon. Jiminy Christmas."

"Okay, lovelies," Cheryl prompted when she stepped out of her office, a single bag slung over her shoulder. "Ready?"

Everyone nodded, but before Gem could take a step, I offered to carry something for them. They looked at me like I'd just threatened to behead their cat.

"I'm not *that* old, little girl."

Before I could tell them I didn't mean any offense, Delaney said, "This girl's sweet, Gem. I was gonna ask if I could hop on your back and let you carry me over there." Delaney looked at me. "They do CrossFit three times a day."

"Three times a *week*," Gem corrected.

"That's what I said." Delaney winked at me.

I was starting to think I might like it there, but it didn't take but a few minutes before I realized that was wishful thinking on my part. When we arrived in the employee lobby, I saw Wayne Parson pacing the floor, and my good mood soured a little. More so when Cheryl marched over to the desk and said something to the security guard before taking what appeared to be a visitor pass. She then strolled over to Wayne and handed it to him.

"From now on, if you can't come prepared, stay home," Cheryl told him before gesturing toward us. "Wayne Parson, meet your new team. Gem Rosen, Delaney Hill, and Journey Zeplyn."

"I think I've died and gone to heaven," Wayne crooned, eye-balling Delaney before those shifty eyes drifted over me. "All these beautiful women."

"I'm not a woman," Gem noted.

Wayne frowned as he openly ogled Gem's chest. "Well, you don't look like a man."

"That's because I'm not."

"Not a man or a woman." He snorted. "What are you then?"

Gem said, "Don't let your idiotic assumptions make you look like an ass."

Too late for that.

Wayne glowered at Gem.

"Team, meet Wayne." Cheryl turned. "This way."

I followed behind her to the double doors. Cheryl opened one of the doors and held it so I could take the handle. I reached for it only to have Wayne practically knock me down as he squeezed past me to get closer to Cheryl.

Looked like chivalry was dead for some.

I held the door for Gem and Delaney, then followed into a large, three-story high atrium complete with a coffee shop and several two-seater tables scattered about. Sunlight flooded through all the glass, making it feel awake and alive. The side opposite the coffee shop overlooked an outdoor area, complete with more tables and filled with a variety of greenery.

We kept walking past another section of offices; these had interior hallways on the second and third floors above. High overhead was a domed skylight that ran the length of the corridor. After that came another community area with more plants and three sets of double doors on the left that led to what could be the cafeteria.

We reached the opposite end and another set of double doors, which Cheryl had to use her badge to unlock.

"Your badge is required to get into this area and onto the elevators."

"Overkill, if you ask me," Wayne muttered.

Cheryl didn't look at him when she added, "It might seem redundant, but it's necessary. If you bring a guest, you must have manager approval, and they will be required to have a visitor badge and to sign in at security before they're permitted to any of the floors. You will be required to escort them at all times. Access is restricted and monitored."

She proved her point when she had Wayne follow her to the security desk, where she had to sign him in. The security guy at this desk was far more thorough, eyeballing Cheryl's badge and requesting Wayne's ID. Once he presented it, the man keyed something into his computer. A minute later, he passed it back, along with another temporary badge Wayne attached to his shirt, followed by a demand that Cheryl accompanies him everywhere he went if he wasn't on our floor. I figured that was why Cheryl told him he should stay home if he didn't come prepared. I doubted our boss wanted to hold his hand everywhere he went.

Once they'd finished, it was over to the elevators with their shiny gold doors. There were two and a door off to the right with a sign for stairs.

Cheryl scanned her badge on the electronic reader, then hit the up button. "Temporary badges won't get you on the elevator," she told Wayne.

"You don't wanna take the stairs?" Delaney teased Gem. "Might be able to skip one of your workouts later."

Gem rolled their eyes, but they looked like they might be smiling. At least on the inside.

"I work out," Wayne acknowledged, brushing his shaggy hair out of his face. "Run about twenty miles a day."

From what I could tell under his loose-fitting Dockers and bright blue polo, Wayne didn't have a runner's physique. He lacked the lower body musculature you'd find in someone who ran religiously. He wasn't overweight, but he wasn't skinny, either.

"Twenty, huh?" Gem didn't sound convinced. "What's your time?"

He considered that for a second. "Just under an hour."

Gem snorted. "My apologies, Usain Bolt. I didn't recognize you."

I couldn't help but grin.

Wayne frowned. "What?"

Gem rolled their eyes again, and thankfully one of the elevator doors opened wide.

Luckily, I was back a few feet because the car wasn't empty, and the two men who exited took up all the space. Well, one of them did, anyway.

Creed Granger and Nick Weston walked forward, continuing their conversation.

I wasn't sure why my breath lodged in my chest, but it did.

"Hey, Nick, Creed. Remember me? I was in the new hire orientation yesterday," Wayne announced a little too loudly.

They both stopped talking, then looked up as though they didn't realize anyone was there. I figured they were used to parting a crowd when they walked, so there was no need to pay attention.

"Good morning, Mr. Granger, Mr. Weston," Cheryl said, a hint of exasperation in her tone.

Nick's gaze locked on Wayne. "Where's your badge?"

Wayne shrugged, casual as you may. "Forgot it at home. I'm not used to having it yet."

"Don't forget it again," Creed stated, his tone as rich and dark as I remembered. "If you do, you're fired."

"He won't, Mr. Granger," Cheryl told him. "Excuse us."

She stepped back and gestured us onto the elevator like we were a group of kindergartners on a field trip.

I stepped forward but not before making eye contact with Creed. When those quicksilver eyes met mine, my heart kicked extra hard in my chest. He held my gaze captive for several heartbeats, and while his expression remained impassive, I swore I saw heat churning in the darkest gray of his eyes.

Nope. I definitely was not imagining that connection I felt yesterday.

"Have a good day," Nick said, a blanket statement aimed at all of us before he smiled at me and urged Creed forward.

6

Journey

I SPENT THE REST OF THE MORNING getting my office set up—an actual office, not just a cubicle like on the floor they had relocated from. It didn't take me long since everything I needed was already set up for me.

Being that I'd never worked in an office setting, I had no expectations when I arrived today, so I was both impressed and surprised by the amount of space there was. Enough to hold a large glossy-white L-shaped desk, matching file cabinet, and bookshelf on one side. The other half of the office was designed for brainstorming—with a small table and three chairs—or perhaps meeting with others, which I figured was vital to the position.

On the desk designed to raise and lower based on the user's preference, there was a Macbook Pro docked to two thirty-two-inch wide-screen monitors, a keyboard, and a trackpad on the drawer that pulled out. It took me a few tries to get the desk to the ergonomically correct height and a few more before I managed to get logged into the secure network. I unpacked the few items I had brought with me. I placed the notebook I used for orientation on the desk along with my favorite gel pens, which I tossed in the small rose-gold cup my mother bought me. And last but not least, the matching phone holder, which I set off to the side along with my cell phone.

The entire time I was working, I could hear Wayne chatting incessantly. I think he took a liking to Delaney because he spent the better part of an hour standing outside her door asking her personal questions. Because she was inside her office, I couldn't hear her responses, but based on her tone, she was a little put out by his forwardness. I couldn't blame her. There was something off about the man.

Once I was done with everything I could do, I offered to help Delaney when the movers delivered her boxes. It took us no time to empty them while she rambled about how cool the new office was. She wasn't wrong.

The community space between our five offices—which formed a U at the end of the floor, with two offices on each side and one at the end—was equally as nice. The open space in the center contained a glossy black conference table with eight rolling chairs, a large glass whiteboard on wheels, and two black leather armchairs spaced out on a large white area rug covered in red and black geometric shapes. Flanking the armchairs were two standing desks that had treadmills beneath them, all set up for someone who didn't want to sit still while they were working. There was also a bean bag chair, a stability ball, a wobble board, and a couple of anti-fatigue mats. All of the equipment had the Primal Instincts logo on them. Prototypes, maybe? Or coming to market? On the opposite end of the sixth floor, there was a setup that mirrored ours, with a breakroom and bathrooms down a hallway that divided the two ends.

After I finished helping Delaney, Cheryl called me into her office, the largest of the five and positioned at the end. Although she had windows, the ocean view was limited due to the height of the neighboring buildings. I sat in one of the two chairs facing her desk while she continued unpacking her things, chattering about her husband of thirty years, their two children, and four grandchildren. She was very proud, and I couldn't say I blamed her. She had a beautiful family and showed them off with all the photos she set up around her office. I liked Cheryl because she reminded me of my mother: a little prim but brimming with pride for the essential things in her life. I considered myself lucky to have a family-oriented boss since family was important to me.

She excused me when her phone rang, so I returned to my office, thankful Wayne had disappeared.

I was sitting at my desk, skimming through the various software applications on my computer, when Cheryl poked her head in an hour later.

"There's a button on the bottom of your desk."

I leaned back in my chair and reached under the desk, gliding my hand along the glossy wood, feeling for it.

"If you click it, the glass will clear."

When I found it, I tapped the small round button and gasped when the glass wall separating me from the community area went from opaque to clear.

Cheryl grinned. "Keep it like that unless you specifically need privacy. That way, I can interrupt without feeling guilty."

I grinned and nodded.

"And in case you haven't found your calendar yet, there's a meeting scheduled from one to four today. Mr. Weston, my boss, would like to take some time to introduce the new people and explain the concept of our team as well as reiterate this year's marketing strategy."

Wow. Three hours to do that?

"I'm looking forward to it," I told her, leaving off the fact that I was a bit intimidated by the idea of a three-hour meeting on my first official day. Eight hours yesterday had far exceeded my quota for the week.

"You want to go to the cafeteria and grab lunch before then?"

Because I liked her, I couldn't come up with a reason not to. The last thing I wanted was to come across as not being a team player, although if I had my way, I'd sneak in a bag of chips at my desk. Plus, I knew I wouldn't be able to accomplish my mission if I spent all my time in my office. I needed to wander; otherwise, I wouldn't uncover the secrets this building contained. Plus, this allowed me to check out the cafeteria since it'd been a hot topic of conversation throughout the morning. Something about breakfast, if I recalled correctly, and I overheard Delaney swooning about lunch.

"I'll tag along if you don't mind."

Well, shit.

"Sure. Come on, Wayne," Cheryl said to the man I thought I was done with after orientation yesterday.

As my luck would have it, not only was he on my team, but Wayne also shared an office wall with me. I knew this because he'd taken every opportunity to bring it up as though the wall was something we had in common, like enjoying sunsets or long walks on the beach.

We took the elevator back to the main floor, listening as Wayne droned on about how gung-ho he was to get a project to work on. Cheryl murmured at appropriate intervals to let him know she was listening.

"Meals are free," Cheryl explained as we stepped into the enormous cafeteria with dozens of small tables and a few larger ones.

Well, that explained all the enthusiasm. Free meals just tasted better.

Cheryl smiled brightly. "Primal Instincts takes care of its employees. Free meals, childcare. You even get a complimentary gym membership to any of our locations. Complete with a personal trainer if you'd like one."

"I get my exercise the old-fashioned way," Wayne chimed in, his eyes zeroed in on me as he winked. "And I definitely don't need childcare. Single. No kids. Got my own place."

Sounded like he was reciting right off his *Match.com* profile.

"Where food is concerned, the options are endless," Cheryl continued as though Wayne hadn't spoken, ticking off the selling points as she smiled over at me. "I've yet to eat anything I didn't like. But I'm picky, so I tend to stick with the basics."

"I'm not," I told her. "Picky, I mean." I didn't tell her that my mother was a fantastic cook, and she tended to experiment with various dishes, mixing and mashing, until she was convinced she'd come up with something no one had ever done before. Then she would hunt it down on the internet, learn she was wrong, and set out to create the next best thing. I think I got my enthusiasm for life from her.

"I'm picky," Wayne noted with an odd cackle. "I prefer blondes."

The guy was ridiculous.

Cheryl led the way through the tables in the dining room toward another area concealed behind intricately detailed walls that you usually only see in a five-star hotel lobby. Past that, the decor ended. What lay beyond looked like every self-serve buffet I'd ever been to, with its various stations dedicated to multiple cuisines. The walls were the same glossy mahogany as the dining space, but everything else was white or stainless steel. The only decor came in the way of interchangeable signs hanging above the stations, signifying what cuisine was there.

Once inside, Cheryl urged Wayne toward the taco bar— bless her—giving me some time to peruse the options.

It all looked good and smelled even better, but I wasn't that hungry, so I opted for a small salad, which I prepared on a glass plate, and a small bowl of the day's soup—pumpkin squash bisque. If there weren't people around, I would've eighty-sixed the soup and salad, snagged a bag of Cheetos puffs and an energy drink, and let the carbs and caffeine fuel me for the rest of the day. Unfortunately, I was looking to develop a professional reputation that didn't include the taste buds of a ten-year-old.

With tray in hand, I made my way to the exit but got sidetracked by the many glass-door refrigerators lining one wall. Intending to get a bottle of water, I paused when I noticed the vast array of energy drinks. I probably didn't need one, but I didn't get one that morning, so the temptation was too great to ignore.

As I stood there scanning the selection, I felt someone move up behind me.

Please don't be Wayne.

"Energy and focus? Or just energy?"

I glanced to my left, relieved to see anyone but Wayne. "I'm sorry?"

Smiling in profile, the man beside me motioned toward the shelves of various colored cans. "Just wondering what's your preference."

I was confused, but not wanting to come off rude, I said, "Focus is as important as energy, right?"

"What's your pleasure?" he offered, opening one of the glass doors.

"Rockstar Zero. Fruit punch, please."

He grabbed the can and a C4 energy drink, then let the door slap shut behind him.

If it were possible, his smile widened as he turned to look my way for the first time, and an involuntary hitch interrupted my breathing. I recognized him instantly but managed to contain my excitement.

While he wasn't traditionally handsome—there wasn't enough symmetry to his face—he was bad-boy gorgeous. He was five feet, ten inches, roughly one hundred seventy pounds. His light brown hair was shaved close to his head, which worked for him, especially since he was clean-shaven. He had a sharp-angled jaw, a blunt chin, a nose that had been broken more than a few times, and there was a long scar above his left eyebrow. Altogether, those minor irregularities added an air of danger to an otherwise ordinary face. But the most fascinating thing about him was that lopsided grin and the gleam of mischief in his ocean-blue eyes.

He shifted everything to one hand and thrust out the other. "Jacob Hawkins. You can call me Hawk."

Somehow I managed to maintain my composure as I balanced my tray on my left arm and shook his proffered hand. "Journey Zeplyn." My composure slipped a little, and I grinned like an idiot. "You're *the* Jacob Hawkins. The world MMA champion. One of the greatest fighters to ever step foot in the octagon."

"You read my resume," he said, his eyes sparkling with amusement, holding my hand for a few seconds longer than was polite in a professional environment.

I knew it was rude to stare, but I couldn't help myself. I was starstruck, but how could I not be? I was a huge fan of MMA, and back when he was fighting, I followed Hawk's career like it was my job. As of the day he retired for medical reasons, his record was 12-1-0, and he was regarded as one of the greatest fighters in MMA history. No doubt, if he hadn't decided to retire, he would've gone on to legendary status.

I knew he was the face of Primal Instincts, but I hadn't realized he actually made appearances in the office. "Do you work here?"

"Every day. Except for Tuesdays." A cocky smirk formed on his mouth. "Tuesdays, I just come for the opportunity to chat about energy drinks with a beautiful woman."

I nodded my chin toward the foil-wrapped food in his hand. "Don't forget the free food."

His blue eyes glittered with what looked like approval. "Definitely the free food."

"Mr. Hawkins?"

I looked behind me to see Cheryl rushing forward, her eyes wide as she glanced between us. Wayne wasn't too far behind her, his forehead creased, expression sour.

"I'm so sorry," she said quickly.

Hawk looked over at Cheryl with a frown. "For?"

My boss peered at me briefly, then turned her concerned gaze back to him. "I didn't realize she'd have questions. I should've been here to answer them."

As I watched my boss stumble with an apology, utter horror etched across her face, I was trying to figure out what was happening. She had done the same thing this morning when Creed and Nick were exiting the elevator. You'd think they were royalty based on her reaction.

Because it was the perfect opening for him to tell me who he was, I waited for Hawk to look at me. He finally did, so I said, "I take it you're not merely a UFC title belt holder with a penchant for energy drink come-ons, are you?"

"Oh, please," Wayne muttered. "What's worse? The fact she doesn't know who he is or that he's *hitting on her* at work."

Cheryl's gaze snapped to Wayne the way a mother did when she expected silence from her annoying kid.

Hawk, ignoring Wayne completely, found my inquiry amusing if his booming laugh meant anything. "Did it work?"

"What?"

"The come-on."

I grinned and shrugged. "It didn't *not* work."

Cheryl inhaled sharply. "Oh, dear heavens."

Hawk looked at my boss and smiled. "It's all right, Cheryl. Journey didn't interrupt me. I approached her."

She put a hand on her chest and exhaled slowly. "Oh, thank God."

He leaned closer to Cheryl, his voice lower when he said, "But if it's all the same to you, I'd like to finish this conversation privately." His eyes slid over my face. "You see, I'm not keen on being mediocre, and not *not* accomplishing something isn't the same as accomplishing it."

"It's a double negative," Wayne noted under his breath. "Of course it's not the same."

Hawk, clearly fed up with Wayne's commentary, looked his way. "When I want your opinion, I'll invite you into the conversation."

Wayne's upper lip curled into a snarl but not until Hawk turned back to me.

"So what do you say, Cheryl? Think I could steal her for a bit?"

When Hawk stepped back, Cheryl's gaze bounced between us. A second later, her eyes went wide as though she was just getting the joke.

Hawk gave her a sideways wink. "I'll ensure she makes it back to her office before her hour's up."

Cheryl nodded, and I wondered how long the shock would take to wear off.

"You should—"

"Quiet, Wayne," Cheryl said, turning away and motioning him toward the exit.

"May I buy you lunch?" Hawk offered when they walked away.

"The *free* lunch?"

A slow smirk curled the corner of his mouth. "That'd be the one, yes."

"Let me guess. You're the type who takes his dates to restaurants that accept coupons," I teased as he put a hand on my lower back and steered me toward the dining room. I pretended that intimate touch didn't light me up from the inside out.

"Only on Mondays," he quipped. "So you're safe for another week."

When I set my tray down on the table to take my seat, Hawk made a show of looking at it closely.

"Is there something wrong with my food?"

He pulled out his chair, eased into it. Using the same tone I'd used a moment ago, he said, "Let me guess. You're the type to eat bird food to impress your date."

I looked at the salad, then back to him. "If this were a date, I would've ordered filet mignon, a baked potato, and cherry cobbler."

"No broccoli?"

I scrunched my nose. "Broccoli's for lightweights."

Hawk clutched a hand to his chest. "A woman after my own heart."

Oh, man, he was a charmer.

I should've probably been nervous about sharing a meal with a man I had just met—a celebrity, to boot—but our unconventional introduction had put me at ease, so I dug in.

"Are you going to tell me who you are"—I waved a hand to encompass the room—"I mean, in this setting … and why my boss acted like I'd committed two of the seven deadly sins at once?"

A slow smirk formed on his mouth. "Which two?"

"I'd go with greed and envy."

His lip quirked a little more. "I was hoping for lust."

"That comes on the second date," I teased. "But you avoided my question."

"Who am I in this setting?" Skepticism made his dark eyebrows angle downward. "You really don't know?"

I casually waved my fork in his direction. "Your face says I should, huh?"

He laughed, flashing another devilish grin. "Have you read the company bio?"

Of course I had. A few dozen times. But if I told him that, he'd think I was a stalker.

I took a bite of my salad, chewed. I waited until I'd swallowed before responding with, "Was it something Nick covered in new hire orientation?"

He was still smiling. "Don't know. Can't say I've had the pleasure."

"If it's not, then no." I laughed. "If it was, then please give my apologies to Nick because I clearly wasn't paying attention."

"You'd be surprised how many women say that about the time they spend with him."

I snorted a laugh. "You'd only tease if you know him. I take it you do."

He peeled the foil from his grilled chicken spinach wrap, took a bite, then said around a mouthful, "We've been introduced."

I took another bite, set down my fork, and opened my energy drink. "I think I need to check out the company bio. And probably that big-ass benefits packet. Clearly, I'm missing some pertinent details."

He sat back in his chair, regarding me with a grin. "I've got time."

I reached into my pocket to grab my phone, only to realize I didn't have it. I must've left it on my desk. Hmm.

"Want to borrow mine?" he asked, holding up his phone as though reading my mind.

"Nah. I'm good." I set the can on the table. "I'll just do some deductive reasoning." I took another bite and considered what I might need to know to figure this out. "You're friends with Nick. Enough that you can undermine his sexual prowess with a joke."

"Sexual prowess, huh?" His grin widened, and his eyebrows rose. "I'll have to tell him someone thinks he has some."

Yeah, I liked this guy. "So that's a yes?"

"Yes, we're friends."

"Okay." I studied him for a moment. "You probably also know Creed Granger."

His eyes glittered with intrigue. "What makes you say that?"

"Yesterday, Creed came to introduce himself to the class. After, he was talking to Nick. They didn't act like two men who only interacted on a professional level. I figure if you know one, you probably know the other. How'm I doing so far?"

"Pretty damn good." A dimple formed in his left cheek. "I'm friends with them both. Deduce something else."

I glanced at the phone in his hand, then back to his face. "You're going to ask for my number." I nodded toward his thumb hovering over the keypad. "Unless you're calling to cancel your previous engagement since I'm far more interesting than Wilhelmina, the girl you took on your coupon date last night."

"It was a two-for-one special," he deadpanned. "I didn't have enough for her, so she had to wait in the car. I don't think she's game for a second date."

I laughed. I couldn't remember the last time I had a meal with a man and felt this at ease. Then again, I didn't have much dating experience to base that on since the last date I went on was to a football game with my high school boyfriend. *In high school.* I didn't bother pursuing anyone during college because it seemed more self-serving to focus all my efforts on getting my degrees.

As I sat there with Hawk, I realized I'd missed out on so much by keeping myself closed off. Had I been more social, perhaps I would've met a hot guy I could banter with a long time ago. Of course, if I had, perhaps I wouldn't be sitting here right now.

"What are you thinking right this second?" Hawk asked, his voice low, his eyes imploring me.

You're witty, fun, and freaking hot. I'm really curious whether your lips are as soft as they look.

I decided to leave off my mental vomit and went with, "That I like you."

Hawk shook his head. "No. That's what *I'm* thinking. You're a mind reader, aren't you?"

"Usually only on Fridays. So this is special. Remember that."

"Trust me; I won't soon forget it." Hawk leaned in closer, his voice even softer than before when he said, "You're fucking adorable, you know that?"

This guy wasn't good for my sanity or my overactive libido. That statement alone made me glad *he* wasn't a mind reader.

7

Creed

A WOMAN'S LAUGHTER CAPTURED MY ATTENTION THE moment I stepped into the employee dining room. I wasn't sure what compelled me to seek out the owner of that laugh, but I did. That was when I saw Hawk and Journey sitting at a table on the far side of the room. They were leaning toward one another like they were engrossed in a titillating conversation, both of them smiling.

Before I even realized I was doing it, I veered off course, heading in their direction rather than going in search of sustenance. I had twenty minutes before my next meeting, which was why I had told Duke I would stop here on the way. But suddenly, food seemed less important than stealing an opportunity to talk to Journey again. Well, speak with her and interrupt whatever the fuck this was that they had going on.

It was bad enough that she had plagued my thoughts since we parted ways last night. With a calendar full of meetings, I figured I would be safe today, better equipped to keep my thoughts from wandering, but that hadn't been the case. Certainly not after our brief encounter in the lobby. Since then, I'd fought the urge to venture to the sixth floor to get another glimpse of her. My self-control had held firm. Until now.

I was watching Hawk as I approached, noticing that he was entering something into his phone. Her number?

Seriously. The guy had no shame.

Her smirk was sex and sin wrapped in a cotton candy package. "Creed."

Yep. I liked how she said my name, and now I was wondering how it would sound on her lips when I made her come.

Journey took a step back to put some distance between us, and I wondered if she was as aware of the heat churning between us as I was.

"I guess I'll see you around."

"You definitely will."

Without another word or a single glance back, Journey headed toward the dining room exit. I stared after her until she disappeared, then turned to Hawk. "Did you have a good lunch?"

He looked as discombobulated as I'd felt last night when I walked her out, his gaze lingering on the doorway. Normally, Hawk would make some snide, possibly crude remark about his intentions for the woman he was just with, but he remained silent, which told me everything I needed to know.

That prediction I made last night ... evidently, I hadn't taken into consideration the appeal of this woman.

However, there was an order to things, and Hawk understood that. Which was why he nodded amenably when I told him there'd be consequences later.

8

Journey

SITTING IN THE CHAIR IN MY CHILDHOOD bedroom, the house completely silent because it was empty, I stared at my computer screen, feeling both giddy and guilty. The former was thanks to the fact I'd shared a meal with an attractive man. And the latter was due to the fact I hadn't been entirely truthful with Hawk about knowing who he was. I hadn't lied exactly, but I had omitted the truth and compounded it by asking him questions.

Fine. I lied.

I exhaled heavily as I stared at the pictures on the bio. Four men made up the top tier of Primal Instincts, LLC, with Creed Granger, the founder and CEO, being the tip of the spear. Then Jacob Hawkins, Nicholas Weston, and Garrison Walker. Garrison was the only one I hadn't met.

My eyes were drawn back to the history of the company and the relationship between the four men who had launched it. They'd been committed to this dream of theirs from the inception of Primal Instincts, the first boxing gym Creed opened back in—*Gah!*—February of 2005. Nineteen months later, they officially opened a second location, this one larger and more impressive. At that point, Nick and Garrison joined the venture into the world of health and fitness alongside Creed. They brought Hawk on as their celebrity endorser in 2013 when he was at the height of his UFC career. He came on board full-time in 2019, just two months after he officially retired from fighting.

In 2005, I was six, and Creed was launching what would become one of the world's most successful fitness companies at the age of twenty-one.

I pushed back from my desk, trying to figure out what all this information did for me. It swirled around in my head as I went downstairs to feed the cats and make myself a sandwich. As soon as I popped the lid on the Fancy Feast, Snowflake, Truffle, and Cinnamon came strolling into the kitchen, looking like the regal divas they were as they somehow managed to stare down their noses at me although they were on the floor, and I was … well … *not*.

"I didn't forget," I assured them, dumping the clumps of food on little saucers and arranging them in a line on the long granite-topped island.

They hopped up, one at a time, like furry little synchronized swimmers. I swore they lifted their little cat eyebrows in that universal expression of *I'm waiting*.

"Spoiled rotten, I tell ya," I muttered before I used the fork to mash the clumps into more pleasing piles.

While they chowed down, I pulled out all the makings for a sandwich. I squirted a generous amount of spicy mustard on two pieces of bread, then layered it with the deli meat my mother kept on hand. I didn't even bother with a plate, figuring it was just one more thing I would have to wash.

I could feel the cats watching me when I squished it together and took a bite.

"You've got your own food," I said around a mouthful. "This is mine."

I ate my sandwich standing up while the cats sat dutifully by in case I dropped something.

As was the case anytime I was there by myself, it felt weird that my parents weren't home, but I was glad they were off enjoying an extended vacation. They'd always said they wanted to travel more for pleasure since most of their trips were business related. I should've known they would eventually give in to the urge. My parents were the type who did what they said they'd do, and they let nothing stand in their way. It was one of many things I truly admired about them.

My cell phone rang as I was washing the cats' plates in the sink. I wrangled it out of my pocket and set it on the counter, then tapped the button to answer the call on speaker as I dried my hands.

"Hey, Mominator," I greeted with a smile.

"How was your day?" she asked without preamble. "Tell me it was better than yesterday."

She was referring to my boring tale of new hire orientation that I had regaled her with last night.

"My ass wasn't numb when I left the building, if that tells you anything."

I purposely left out that I had lunch with a celebrity and joked with the company owner, instead choosing to tell her about meeting my new team and boss. I also omitted Wayne's overzealousness and the fact I'd contemplated filling his office with noxious gas to get him to leave me alone.

"Sounds like you had a good day."

"I did." And despite not knowing what to make of my interactions with Creed and Hawk, it was true.

"I'm glad." My mom sounded pleased. "And you like your boss. That's promising."

"It is. What about you?" I asked. "How's the trip?"

Her tone was wistful when she said, "We really needed this time just for us."

"I take it Bank and Wallet aren't putting up too much of a fight?"

No, I didn't call my parents by common parental names, but my parents weren't standard in any way. I'd come up with some doozies over the years, but Bank and Wallet were my faves for the dads. And rather apropos at the moment, considering the money they had forked out to help me get my apartment.

Turned out, the going rate for a one-bedroom apartment in L.A. was the equivalent of tuition at a top-tier school. My grand plan of shaking that trust-fund-baby stigma backfired when I caved to my parents' demands: gated complex, armed security, third floor. Those were just what I had to agree to in order to avoid having them visit every day to check on me. To pull it off, I had to let them pay the security deposit plus the first and last months' rent since my job at Starbucks barely afforded me the basics required to simply commute in California.

And yes, I really had worked at Starbucks after college—albeit very briefly—although my parents had tons of money and lived in the Hollywood Hills. I didn't have to get a job for financial reasons, but I did have to do it for my sanity.

My mom laughed softly. "Do they ever?"

Did I mention I had two dads? Probably not. It wasn't something I thought about when referring to my parents. Some people had a mom and dad, some had two moms, and others had two dads. I knew a girl in high school who had two moms and one dad, but she always referred to him as the sperm donor, so it wasn't the same thing.

Most people who met my parents didn't know what to make of their relationship, but it only took a short time in their company before the question of how my mother ended up married—in all ways that counted, except legally—to identical twins became a non-issue. Cadence Clearwater met Roman and Ryder Zeplyn in October 1994, three years before I was conceived. And to hear my fathers tell it, the instant they laid eyes on the fair-haired eighteen-year-old college freshman, it was love at first sight. For both of them.

"Y'all still planning to be gone until the seventeenth?" I asked, wondering if I could wait another ten days before I blurted out the tawdry details of my first couple of days at work. My mom would find it amusing that I opened my mouth and inserted both feet with the CEO and one of the VPs of the company I worked for. And once she commended me for that, she'd want to know if I was dating either of them—or both.

My mother chuckled. "Your Texas is shinin' through."

I smiled. She was referring to my use of *y'all*, something I hadn't been able to break despite the fact we moved to California when I was twelve.

"If not Friday, then early Saturday morning," she continued. "Ryder wants to stay in Chicago for an extra day."

"To see Millenium Park? Or Navy Pier?"

"Who knows with them," she answered.

That told me there was another attraction they were seeking—one they didn't want me to know about. Since Chicago was home to Dichotomy, one of the most infamous BDSM clubs in the world, there was a better than fair chance that was the attraction they were visiting.

While my parents were great at a lot of things, they hadn't mastered the art of keeping me in the dark. They hid their secrets well, but I was admittedly a nosy girl, had been all my life. They were part of the reason I started this quest to unearth the secrets behind Primal Instincts in the first place. Not that I would ever tell them that. The less they knew, the better.

"Have fun and be careful," I said.

"We will. Now go, enjoy your evening and get some rest. The week's not half over yet."

We said our *I love you*s then the call disconnected. I finished in the kitchen, turned off the lights, and headed upstairs. Because it allowed me to sleep in longer, I opted for a shower, then grabbed my laptop and took a seat in the bubble chair my dads made for me when I was a kid.

I got settled, opened my laptop, and pulled up my favorite social media site. It wasn't one that most people were signed up for, but it was quite popular in certain circles—namely, the kink crowd.

It was my interest in BDSM that brought me to this particular site several years ago, and since discovering its existence, I hadn't been the same. In fact, it was where I met Rhylee and Avery, my two closest friends. We were stumbling over each other in our comments on someone else's post. I couldn't remember what it was about, but that had kicked off our friendship, and since then, we'd become inseparable, despite the fact we'd been scattered across the country at the time. I'd been in New Jersey at Princeton, Avery in Florida, and Rhylee here in California. Now that I was back here, Rhylee and I were neighbors. Literally. She lived in the same apartment complex I did. As for Avery, she was still in Florida, but she swore she was moving here the first chance she got.

I clicked the link for the comments on my post from last night, noticing there were fifty-two new ones. With a sigh, I started skimming through them. Although it was the least favorite part of my day, it was a necessary evil because some people didn't understand boundaries. And even in the kink community, there were boundaries.

Let me preface this by saying I wasn't a writer, nor did I have any aspirations to be one. However, as it turned out, I was pretty good at penning a short story. It started when Rhylee dared me to post something provocative and dirty. On this site, that could be anything from nude photos to poetry to … well, the imagination knows no bounds. I chose to write out a fantasy and posted it thinking it would get lost in the never-ending newsfeed like everything else. It got some attention and more than a few requests for me to write more. So I did, and I tagged it with *#GuiltyPleasures*. These days, I wasn't the only one who wrote erotic short stories, utilizing the hashtag to get visibility.

My profile was not me, per se, but more like a fictitious me—a more outgoing and daring version of myself. I didn't use my real name, instead utilizing the creative pseudonym JoZe to protect my anonymity. I didn't post pictures of myself or anything that might give away my location. Nor did I interact with most of the people who messaged me. As with any online personality, I had my fair share of trolls who liked to leave disturbing comments, so I was forced to skim them so I could delete or report those that creeped me out.

This site's biggest downfall was that dick pics were abundant, even when you didn't request them. But the pics were the least of my worries. It was the comments that often made me cringe. Like this one: *You're a dirty, filthy slut. One of these days, I'm going to help you out and bring your rape fantasy to life.*

Well, for starters, I didn't have a rape fantasy, and nothing in my writing would make anyone believe otherwise.

I clicked the *hide* button beside the comment and effectively removed it, then blocked their profile for good measure. Not that it mattered. New profiles showed up daily, and since my profile wasn't set to private, anyone could comment.

I wouldn't go so far as to say writing was a hobby for me. I wrote because I enjoyed it and because it cleared the thoughts from my head. If I put it on the page, it was set free forever, so I tended not to dwell. And while my stories were generally based on real people, I always changed their names to protect the innocent. I seriously doubted the hot guy who worked in the deli at the grocery store would appreciate knowing I had fantasized about him having his wicked way with me in the backseat of his Nissan a few weeks ago. I mean, he was probably married.

I removed all the negativity from the comments, opened my writing app, then leaned back and stared at the blank screen. I knew exactly what was going on the page today. Since last night's story involved an über-sexy CEO, who walked into the recently released new-hire orientation and seduced me with his gruff baritone and stormy gray eyes, tonight's would be about a sinful UFC fighter using discretion to make me come in interesting ways while sitting in a room full of people.

Perhaps I should feel guilty that I was fantasizing about two different men. I didn't. Not even a little. It wasn't my fault popular contemporary romance novels depicted relationships as between two people. I wasn't a contemporary girl; therefore, I wasn't looking for a contemporary romance. I wanted something outside the box, something worthy of my fantasies.

Stretching my fingers, I smiled at the screen. As soon as my fingers touched the keyboard, my latest fantasy came to life on the page.

Forty-five minutes later, as I was deep in my fictional world, my fingers flying over the keyboard, my cell phone chimed. It pulled me right out of the zone.

I figured it was my mother messaging to say goodnight, despite the fact I had spoken with her a little while ago. She did that. My mother worried about me, even if she knew where I was and what I was doing.

Closing my laptop, I set it aside and hopped to my feet. I grabbed my phone from where I had left it on the desk, smiling as I recalled the story I'd been immersed in. It had heated up quickly, but that seemed to be the case anytime I sat down to write these days.

I glanced at the phone screen and saw I had a text message from a number that wasn't in my address book.

As I carried the phone back to my reading chair, a smile formed when I read the message.

💬 I ENJOYED LUNCH TODAY. JUST WONDERING IF YOU'D BE UP FOR DOING IT AGAIN SOMETIME SOON.

Hawk.

It had to be.

Honestly, I wasn't expecting him to text or call, figuring his acquiring my number was just part of the flirting routine we'd engaged in.

💬 DEPENDS ON WHETHER YOU EXPECT ME TO PICK UP THE TAB NEXT TIME.

I hit send and stared at my message, immediately breaking it down and wondering whether it was too flirty or not enough. You know how it went. All the questions you asked yourself when you met someone and wanted to get to know them better, only you had no idea what to say or how it would come across.

The three bouncing dots appeared, signaling he was responding, so I shoved away all the insecurities. I had no reason to be nervous, right? I met a man, we shared a meal, and we laughed a lot. It couldn't have gone better.

Well, with the exception of Creed's appearance. When he arrived, it was a wonder I didn't go up in flames. I felt like I'd been caught red-handed doing something I shouldn't. I thought I played it off rather well. The last thing I recalled was discreetly peering back to see both of them watching as I exited the cafeteria. I won't lie; I liked that they were.

My phone buzzed, drawing my attention.

💬 HOW ABOUT COFFEE? AT THE OFFICE TOMORROW. WHAT TIME DO YOU HAVE TO BE THERE?

A giddy sensation bubbled in my belly at the thought of seeing him again.

> 💬 I'D LIKE THAT. I HAVE TO BE THERE AT EIGHT.

💬 DOES SEVEN WORK?

> 💬 SEVEN'S PERFECT.

💬 I LOOK FORWARD TO SEEING YOU AT SEVEN. HOW DO YOU TAKE YOUR COFFEE?

> 💬 IN THE FORM OF A CARAMEL MACCHIATO.

💬 😄 OF COURSE YOU DO. SWEET, STRONG, AND UNCOMPLICATED. I LIKE THAT IN A WOMAN.

> 💬 I FORGOT TO ADD NONFAT MILK WITH WHIPPED CREAM AND AN EXTRA SHOT OF ESPRESSO. HOW'S THAT FOR UNCOMPLICATED?

💬 I'M NOTHING IF NOT ADAPTABLE. SEE YOU AT SEVEN. LOOKING FORWARD TO IT.

> 💬 ME, TOO.

When I went to sleep an hour later, I dreamed about an uber-sexy CEO *and* a prizefighter, only in my dream, they weren't texting me, but there were a lot of fingers working.

9

Creed

"YOUR TIMING'S IMPECCABLE," I TOLD GARRISON WHEN he came through the front door a little after nine.

I'd been anticipating his arrival for the past hour, hoping he would be delayed.

"Where is he?" Garrison asked, glancing around the living room as though expecting to see Hawk chained to one of the walls.

"Downstairs." I set my iPad aside and picked up my bourbon.

Garrison glanced at the iPad and smirked. "You've been watchin' him."

I didn't bother commenting. We both knew I was. There was no denying I was a voyeur, but that was only one of my many kinks. However, in this instance, I wasn't watching to stir my libido; I was watching to ensure Hawk wasn't attempting to get free. He was squirrelly like that. There had been times I had tied him down, convinced there was no possible way he could get free, only to find him stalking me a short while later, grinning and eager for the punishment it earned him.

And fine, I *was* watching Hawk for selfish reasons but against my better judgment. And since I'd been down that road before, I refused to do it again. Hence the reason Garrison was there.

"Shall I tend to him?" Garrison prompted, meeting my gaze.

"In due time," I told him as I got to my feet and headed for the decanter to refill my glass. I offered Garrison one, but he politely declined, waiting patiently for me to lead the way downstairs.

It'd been seven months since I had punished Hawk for one of his many transgressions. I refrained for two reasons. One, Hawk would prefer I was the one doling out his punishment, and two, I would prefer it as well. Since our falling out, I had managed to keep my distance, and I knew the moment I took over punishing him, keeping my hands off him would be damn near impossible.

Most of the time, I'd send Garrison in alone to handle Hawk, but tonight, I wanted a firsthand account of the punishment. After all, it was part of the appeal of my lifestyle. And ultimately, it was one of the reasons Hawk was the way he was. The man liked to push boundaries. More specifically, he liked to push me. Especially when I was helpless to do anything about it. After all, it wasn't like I could address him where unsuspecting witnesses might question my tactics.

The type of punishment I utilized varied. I wasn't a Sadist, so it wasn't about inflicting pain to get off. I preferred rough play—*really* rough, if you wanted to get technical—as opposed to inflicting pain. I would deliver it when the situation warranted, but generally only when earned and occasionally to enhance pleasure.

I took another sip and resigned myself to the encounter. I motioned for Garrison to follow me as I headed for the storage space behind the butler's pantry.

When I first looked at this house three years ago, I wasn't sure what I was looking for. As a newly-minted billionaire at the time, my options were endless, and admittedly, I'd been going for extravagant. What I ended up with couldn't have been more perfect. With twenty thousand square feet, the majority of it designed around entertaining, I couldn't have imagined anything better. One of my favorite rooms happened to be the wine cellar, which the previous owners had been renovating before they foreclosed. They'd laid stone pavers across the floor and carried the theme up the walls and across the ceiling. It was a direct contrast to the modern architecture of the house, and most people would've considered it hideous. The enthusiastic real estate agent had tried to fill my head with promises of superfluous design. After all, when money was no object, grandeur was on the menu. I didn't bother telling him it was perfect exactly as it was: completely bare and large enough to hold the equipment needed to punish the most unruly submissive.

We descended the short staircase, neither of us speaking.

Because the previous owners had intended to show off their collection, the door to the room was made of glass, which offered an unobstructed view of the man currently shackled to the wall at the opposite end. I pulled open the door and gestured Garrison inside. The lights were dimmed to the point it required me to squint to see that Hawk's lean, muscular frame was as rigid as his jaw. The only sound came from the machine attached to his dick, constantly milking him close to orgasm but stopping just short of giving him relief. By design, of course.

Hawk grunted as we approached but didn't say a word. Then again, he couldn't because of the ball gag stretching his lips wide.

Garrison chuckled, openly admiring the man experiencing the fine art of edging, one of my specialties. "How much of a head start did you give him?"

"Two minutes."

"Nice work. What did he do this time?"

"He had lunch with Journey today."

84

Garrison smirked as he released the buttons on his shirt cuffs. "Well, the rule in the office is to engage as a vanilla would."

True. That was our rule. Most of the time, I could let shit slide. However, I had specifically stated she was off limits. Seeing Hawk having lunch in the office cafeteria and openly flirting with her triggered that primal, ingrained need for self-preservation. As far as I was concerned, punishment was the only recourse to satisfy me.

"In a way, this is a good thing," Garrison mused, watching Hawk as he freed the buttons down the front of his shirt. "He's gotten you an in with her, at least."

We both knew I didn't need help in that regard. Based on my brief interactions with Journey, I'd piqued her interest without Hawk's help. Granted, he had likely progressed things along faster than I would have.

"And because of that, I will allow him to come," I informed Garrison.

Hawk grunted again, his eyes narrowed as he tried to bite down on the rubber ball keeping him from speaking. He was panting in earnest now, the machine pulsing and suctioning to his dick again.

"But not yet," I growled roughly.

Hawk groaned, his head falling back against the stone wall.

"First, he needs to be reminded of the hierarchy," I stated before glancing at Garrison. "That's where you come in."

Garrison's smile was slow and devious, his shirt coming off to reveal his impressive upper body. "Anything specific you'd like me to do to him?"

"Make it hurt."

"It would be my pleasure."

10

Jacob "Hawk" Hawkins

PUNISHMENT: MY ABSOLUTE LEAST FAVORITE THING.
Fucking: the reason I earn punishment.

Whenever Creed mentioned the hierarchy, those were the first things that came to mind.

It'd been nearly a decade since I'd been introduced to Creed's primal hierarchy and the rules outlined by the lifestyle he lived. I knew it backward and forward because I'd pushed every boundary I could in my efforts to break the man. Even as I stood there, chained to the fucking wall, forced to endure the humiliation of having a machine milking my dick and a fucking ball shoved in my mouth, I was coming up with new ways to push him, to see if I could crack that granite-hard exterior. Even the slightest fissure would disprove the theory that Creed Granger could not be broken.

One day.

For now, my only job was to endure whatever he had in store for me. Or rather, whatever Garrison had in store.

While punishment was my least favorite thing, I learned to use it to my benefit. Not at first, of course. Hell, back when I first met them and learned about the kinky shit they were into, I outright pledged that I would never get mixed up in shit like that. I probably even declared you would never find me in the exact position I was in now.

It took one trip to the club, just a few hours of watching Creed, Garrison, and Nick succumbing to their baser instincts, and I was hooked. Two years after that, I was experimenting with things I didn't even know were *things*. Those riveting encounters introduced me to a world filled with pain and pleasure that shifted my focus in an entirely different direction.

I watched Garrison as he approached. The guy was a walking wet dream. Six feet, two inches of breathtaking masculinity. Two hundred pounds of solid muscle. A living, breathing work of art, and that was without a single tattoo marring all that sun-bronzed skin covering the ripple of muscles beneath. Even the way he walked—with a slightly bow-legged swagger—was hot as fuck.

A decade ago, if someone had told me my dick would one day get hard by looking at a man, I would've told them to get fucked.

If they'd told me I'd be naked and shackled to a stone wall, a ball gag shoved in my mouth while drool ran down my chin and chest, and a machine jerked me off, I would've told them to get double fucked.

Yet here I was.

Then again, ten years ago, I was just a wide-eyed dreamer getting the hell beat out of me for a shit-ton of money. I was two years into a career that would introduce me to money, women, and power, the likes of which I hadn't known existed. A career that had stemmed from years of being bullied in school by kids who were bigger but never smarter. My old man was a bastard of the highest order, but I did have to thank him for enrolling me in my first karate class when I was eight years old. Needless to say, the bullying and the beatings only lasted so long after that.

These days, I endured my fair share of beatings, but they were consensual and generally resulted in me getting fucked. Unfortunately, we hadn't made it that far in tonight's main event. However, my dick was getting more attention than I cared for, thanks to the milking machine Creed had hooked me up to.

The machine attached to my dick sounded like the air compressor on a semi when the air brakes were engaged, as it quite literally milked me. There was a harness strapped around my hips, which held a rubber-lined tube that my cock was shoved into. It was well-lubricated, so it wasn't as bad as it sounded. The torture came when the machine was turned on. The hoses attached caused the tube to create a vacuum that pulsated and sucked. At first, it was exquisite. It wasn't the same as having a mouth on your dick, but it stimulated in much the same way. If I were allowed to come, it would've been my favorite fucking toy in the house. Since I wasn't, I'd spent more than my fair share of time cursing the fucking thing to hell and back.

The first time Creed put it on me, I came within a minute. The second time was two minutes. Then he introduced me to edging, which was exactly what the name implied. It was a process of bringing someone right to the edge of orgasm over and over, but thanks to Creed's penchant for orgasm denial, there was rarely a happy ending. It had taken him years to train me to get to the point where I could come on command, as well as multiple times if he saw fit. My record was four times in three hours. By the third time, it lacked enjoyment. The fourth time was agony. Yes, because Creed was such a formidable teacher, I could pretty much come without thinking about it, but I didn't because I'd learned that the repercussions for that weren't worth those few seconds of relief.

And here we were.

For the record, chaining me to the wall wasn't an easy task. I didn't go willingly. Ever. I would endure if and when Creed caught me, which he did every single time. The man was determined; I'd give him that. These days, Creed handled the pursuit while Garrison was in charge of the punishment. I'd suffered more at Garrison's hands than I cared to admit, but only because it spoke to my recalcitrant nature. I was a rule breaker; anyone would tell you that. I found any reason to defy authority because I could.

Some would label me as submissive, but I wasn't. Although I lived the lifestyle full-time, there was no way to categorize my contributions. I wasn't a Dominant, nor was I a submissive, yet somehow I fit into their world the same as they did.

These days I spent most of my time in the role of prey, as Creed and Garrison liked to refer to me. It wasn't a role many people would volunteer for, especially when Primal Doms like Creed and Garrison got too much enjoyment from playing with their food. I didn't mind because I found great pleasure in pushing Creed's buttons simply to get a rise out of him. And also because it resulted in sessions such as this one. I enjoyed the attention that came along with the pain Creed saw fit to inflict on me. Which I figured was the main reason Creed had been farming out my punishment to Garrison. It was two-fold in that what I wanted most— Creed's attention—was kept from me, *and* I had to endure whatever sadistic idea Garrison had come up with. And the man could come up with some fucking doozies.

"I got somethin' special for you," Garrison drawled as he strolled toward me.

He slid his hand into his jeans pocket and pulled out something red. I couldn't make out what it was, but I was sure I wouldn't like it.

"Let's get this off you first," he said, setting the red triangle-shaped thing on the table. It was close enough that I could see it, but identifying what it was used for was nearly impossible. I figured that was part of Garrison's mental manipulation. He knew I would fret over what was in store for me while he worked to free my cock from the milking machine.

That was exactly what I did. The red thing looked like rubber molded into an inverted triangle shape; only the bottom point wasn't connected. A hole in the center was about two fingers wide, and because the base point was not connected, it could be stretched open. The inside of the circle had black raised ridges that looked—

Son of a bitch.

Garrison chuckled as though he could read my mind and knew I'd figured it out. "I know how much you like e-stim."

Electrical stimulation.

I moaned around the ball gag.

Garrison grinned. "Don't worry. Creed said you could come. I'll fuck you hard enough to ensure that happens."

Perhaps I could suffer through having electricity arcing through my dick and balls if it meant Garrison was going to rail me. It had felt like an eternity since I was last fucked properly.

While he unstrapped the harness, I considered it but decided no, not even the promise of Garrison's cock tunneling in and out of my ass was enough to keep my dick hard. In fact, the damn thing was shriveling without the machine.

Garrison reached around to unhook the strap holding the ball gag in place. His mouth was close to my ear when he said, "Maybe if you're really good, Creed will fuck you, too."

Now, *that* was enough to make my cock swell, even though I knew it wouldn't happen. Creed hadn't fucked me in seven months, and he'd told me in no uncertain terms that he never would again. I believed him.

Because Garrison knew I would run the moment there was an opportunity, he connected a thick metal collar around my neck and attached it to a short chain, which he wrapped tightly around his fist. He dragged me across the room because I made him work for it. Eventually, he managed to subdue me, connecting the chain to one dangling from the ceiling, preventing me from getting away.

With me still fighting him, Garrison positioned me in his favorite place—the leather sling. It was pretty basic, as was most of the play furniture we owned. The leather sling was roughly the length from my neck to my ass and was connected by thick-gauge chains hooked to mounts in the ceiling. Using a pulley system, it could be raised and lowered, as could the wrist and ankle cuffs, separately or together. Meaning Garrison could get really fucking creative with how he positioned me if he wanted to.

"You want him in a specific position?" Garrison asked Creed.

"As uncomfortable as possible," he answered without an ounce of emotion.

Garrison granted him his wish, connecting the metal cuffs to my wrists and ankles, then connecting them with D-links to the chains hanging from the ceiling. He adjusted everything so I was on my back in the sling, tipped at an angle so that my head was dangling mere inches above the concrete floor, ass high, knees near my shoulders, legs wide, and secured by a large leather strap that wrapped across the back of my thighs close to my knees and beneath me, secured with more hooks.

Imagine the fetal position only dangling in midair.

Like that, Garrison had easy access to my ass and my dick which allowed him to connect the contraption to my cock. For the next few minutes, Garrison went through the motions, attaching the silicone cock ring at the base of my cock, the unconnected point tucked behind my balls. It wasn't uncomfortable, but I couldn't relax because I knew it would send shocks through my dick. Wires were connected next to give it the *umph* intended.

I had no control over anything he did, nor could I see what he was doing. There were no mirrors in this space, no reflective glass. Nothing that might've given me an idea of what he would do next. To top it off, he turned on the stereo, blasting "Black Soul" by Shinedown. It was fitting, both for me and the situation.

Accepting that I wasn't getting out of this, I focused on breathing, closing my eyes, feeling the song as it moved through the space. The first shock to my dick made me grunt. Not so much from pain but surprise. It wasn't uncomfortable. Not yet. I'd had more electric stimulation to my muscles via a TENS unit.

Of course, I spoke far too soon. The lubricant left behind from the milking machine acted as a perfect conduit for the electricity. Garrison controlled the stimulation with a remote, and the intensity increased as the minutes ticked by until my dick was spasming from the electric pulses.

When the third song began, Garrison made it significantly worse as he stretched my ass open with two well-lubed fingers. He was almost gentle, which directly conflicted with the pain radiating between my legs.

By the time the fifth song began, I was groaning, the muscles in my neck spasming as the electric current shooting through my dick caused my entire body to tense. The stimulation was maintained at my groin, but the sensation moved through me like every limb was plugged into a wall socket. It was made intensely worse thanks to the vibrating toy Garrison shoved in my ass and was holding directly on my prostate.

I didn't cry out, but I wanted to.

I didn't beg him to stop, although I wanted to do that, too.

I'd take whatever he wanted to give me because Creed demanded it. I would never promise Creed that I'd obey. He knew I wouldn't. But I would always endure my punishment.

I just hoped he'd be lenient next time since this was my punishment for having lunch with Journey. I could only imagine what he would come up with when he found out I was having coffee with her tomorrow morning. We would find out soon enough, but those few minutes I would get with her … yeah, it made every second of this worth it.

"You ready for me?" Garrison growled softly when the room went eerily silent.

I didn't answer him, instead taking deep, cleansing breaths when the electricity and the brutal vibration disappeared.

I inhaled long and slow when Garrison pressed his cock against my ass. Thank God he had worked me open with that fucking vibrator because he wasn't gentle when he rammed his thick cock inside me. I gritted my teeth and grunted through the pain. It was so fucking good, but I didn't let him know that. I couldn't stand it if he stopped fucking me. It was what kept me going.

"Fuck," Garrison hissed when he pulled the chains, jerking me toward him and impaling me on his cock. "You're stranglin' my dick. Fuck, you're tight. Take every inch, Hawk. Let me in."

He wasn't gentle. He never was. It was what I liked about him. He took his pleasure from me however he saw fit. He used me, but he always *always* made sure I was aware he was the one fucking me. I wasn't a nameless orifice he was using to sate the urge. He might've signed up to punish me, but I knew there was more behind it than that.

As he began to fuck me harder, the pleasure overrode all the pain. I savored every second, holding off until Garrison permitted me to come.

And when it was over, after Garrison had freed me from the restraints and I could sit up, I experienced the worst punishment of all.

Creed wasn't there.

He hadn't watched a goddamn thing.

11

Journey

THE FOLLOWING DAY, I WAS UP BEFORE my alarm went off.

With my shower out of the way last night, it didn't take long to get ready. I spent a few minutes on my makeup, straightening my hair, and trying to decide which of the few clothes I'd brought with me would work best for both work and an impromptu date. I decided on a black silk button-up blouse with an open neckline and a short gray plaid skirt. I paired the outfit with knee-high suede boots instead of heels to dress it down a little.

Once I was finished, I had enough time to feed the cats, clean their plates, and grab my bag, keys, and security badge to get me into the building before I was out the door and on my way to the office.

When I arrived, I badged in through the employee entrance, then showed my badge to Kurt, whom I greeted by name. He waved me on with a smile.

I headed for the coffee shop in the atrium. Despite the early hour, there were a few people already there. Two in line, another pair sitting at a table appearing to be engrossed in a conversation over a laptop, and another guy pacing back and forth, phone to his ear. But the one who caught my eye was the handsome former MMA fighter at a table by the wall of windows overlooking the courtyard. His expression softened when he saw me, and a sinful smirk appeared.

"Good morning," I greeted as Hawk got to his feet, his eyes skimming over me from head to toe.

"It definitely is."

Like yesterday, he was wearing a pair of jeans, but instead of a collared polo, he had on a navy blue Henley that accentuated his blue eyes. The sleeves were pushed up to his elbows, revealing thick forearms and the dusting of hair that covered them. There was a tattoo on the inside of his right forearm, but I couldn't make out what it was because of the position of his arm.

"Did you sleep well?" he asked as we took our seats.

I set my bag on the floor by my feet and met his gaze. "Maybe," I said, scrunching my nose. "I'm not sure. I kept having this dream."

He nodded as though it made perfect sense. "I tend to do that to women. It happens whenever they meet me."

I didn't bother telling him my dream entailed two sinfully hot men. He would likely think that was awkward.

I laughed as I took a sip of my coffee. "Oh, really?"

"Oh, yeah." He aimed for serious, but there was mischief glittering in his eyes. "It's my charm and my boyish good looks. Women can't resist me."

Yeah, he was definitely irresistible. I'd certainly spent a lot of time swooning over this delectable bad boy.

"Is that right?" I teased.

"Well, it could also be the gift I have."

"Gift?" I smiled wide, wanting him to elaborate. "Do tell."

"I try not to make a big deal out of it, but I've got this mind-melding ability. I can slip right in and control your thoughts. I did it yesterday at lunch."

"Did you?"

His grin turned wicked, and it changed his appearance in ways that should be illegal. "I did." He shook his head. "Now that I've done it … it's inevitable. You're gonna fall in love with me." He scrunched his nose. "You probably already are."

I fluttered a hand, unable to control the ridiculous smile on my face. "Oh, well, if that's all."

He leaned back, nodding his head as though accepting a hard truth. "It's cool, though. I don't mind."

"You won't mind if I'm in love with you?" A laugh/snort escaped, but I was too amused by his charm to be embarrassed.

"It was bound to happen sooner or later." His eyes narrowed, still glittering with amusement. "You don't mind, do you?"

"Oh, not at all." I relaxed. "I prefer to move things at warp speed. No need to fuss over all those little courting rituals."

"I'll still court you," he said as he picked up his coffee. "I figure coffee this morning, dinner tomorrow, by the weekend, we'll be making our way to Vegas. We can be married by an Elvis impersonator. I hear they're all the rage."

I laughed. "I've heard that, too. Plus, it sets a precedent for the marriage, right?"

"Most definitely. Lots of gyrating hips and snarling lips in our future."

And to think, I was worried we wouldn't have anything to talk about.

Two hours later, my morning was well underway, and I still had a smile on my face despite the fact I'd had to deal with Wayne's inappropriate comments about my outfit. Evidently, he believed slacks were the better way to go when it came to business attire for women. Yes. Those were his words. He had the audacity to tell me I should take a page from Gem's book and go for the androgynous look.

I took offense to his statement not only for myself but also for Gem. How we dressed was none of his concern. Or anyone's, for that matter. Unfortunately, Wayne did not seem to recognize body language because he carried on as though I had sought him out personally for fashion advice. I wondered if he even realized the more he spoke, the stupider he sounded.

"Are you ready for this?"

The question came from Delaney as we made our way to a conference room on the third floor of the executive building. Apparently, it was where they had meetings when the top-level execs were expected to appear.

I passed her a small smile hoping not to convey the anxiety coursing through my veins. I had no idea whether Creed or Hawk would be in attendance, but even the minute possibility made my stomach quiver. Since Cheryl specifically said top-level, they were the only ones I could think about.

"Don't worry; I hear they don't put the new people on the spot," she added as we took the elevator down.

She wasn't helping, but I didn't think she was aware of that because her eyes were laughing, and her gait was far too chipper. Or it was possible she was enjoying making me squirm. If she only knew the reason had nothing to do with my capability regarding my job but more so from the interactions I'd had with a couple of people who might or might not be in this meeting.

"If they need help from anyone, I'm sure they'll call on me," Wayne chimed in behind us. "But you two can stand around and look pretty. That's always a bonus."

Misogynistic prick.

"Jackass," Delaney muttered under her breath, her good mood vanishing like mine had earlier.

We were silent as we made our way to the conference room, then inside, where there was a large U-shaped table designed the same as the orientation room. On the wall was an eighty-five-inch television used for presentations.

"Spread out," Cheryl said when she strolled in behind us. "One on each side, two at the back."

When Wayne grabbed a chair closest to the door, I moved to the far side of the room while Delaney went opposite me. That left Gem having to sit at the same table with Wayne, but I figured if anyone could handle him, it'd be them.

"This meeting has been a long time coming," Cheryl prompted as she connected her laptop to one of the cords on the table. "In case you don't know, we had our annual trade show back in October. During that event, we surveyed those who visited our booth and combined the responses with one we ran on the website for the last two months of the year."

She grabbed a remote control and clicked a button. The screen brightened with an image of the Primal Instincts logo. The symbol they used was the uruz rune, which I had to look up when I first saw it. The uruz rune symbolized many things based on various interpretations from Norse mythology, an ancient Germanic alphabet, and others. The most common translations were vitality, strength, and raw energy. It was often a symbol of power and ferocity and was used by those who identified with primal instincts. Which, I figured, was how they came up with it.

"Why did they use an awkwardly shaped N as their logo?" Wayne asked.

"It's the uruz rune," Gem corrected.

Wayne frowned. "That means nothing to me."

Gem rolled their eyes.

"I suggest you read the backstory on the website," Cheryl said, interrupting before a fight could ensue. "There's a lot of detailed information about how the company came to be." She clicked the remote. "Moving on."

The screen changed to show four boxes, each with a title—CBD, Reflect, fitness tracker, and rowing machine—and a few words to describe each.

"These are the top four products our customers are interested in. Outside of what we already have, anyway. The objective of this meeting is to determine who will be taking which product. Our product design teams are well underway on these and several others and have been for a while now. Thanks to the surveys, we've narrowed our focus to four and will put all our marketing efforts behind them for a rollout by the end of the year."

Cheryl looked to the back of the room and waved someone forward.

For the next hour and a half, we listened to the product management team leaders as they walked through their respective categories, providing a high-level overview of each product. It was apparent they each had a vested interest in the success of their product, most importantly with the launch.

Once they'd all completed their presentations, I found myself holding my breath, hoping Creed or Hawk wouldn't come in, while at the same time, wishing they would.

Cheryl waited until they'd left the room before turning to us again. "Now for the fun part. Assigning the products to the team."

"I'll take the rowing machine," Wayne said, lifting a finger like he was bidding in an auction.

"That will not be up to you to decide," Cheryl said smoothly. "For the rest of this week, I want you to research each of these products. Talk to the product development teams, look at the prototypes they've created, and review the workups and project boards. As you heard, each team is very passionate about their product, and they won't hesitate to tell you why.

"Do not focus solely on one because there's no guarantee you'll be chosen to market that product. On Tuesday of next week, you'll present to me, and we'll walk through how you'll present to the directors. From there, they'll suggest who they think will benefit their launch. After that, you'll present to the VPs and the CEO to walk them through your ideas for rollout."

Cheryl had me right up until the last sentence. I loved the idea. Having the opportunity to research each product and learn more about it rather than being assigned one allowed us to find something that suited our personalities. Sure, I was confident I could handle the brand management of anything they tossed my way, but I was excited to see if one appealed to me over the other.

However, presenting to Creed and the VPs was a terrifying prospect considering our interactions thus far.

Cheryl said, "In case you'd like to attend, there's an executive-level meeting this afternoon regarding the line of CBD products they've developed. It's probably a good place to start for that one."

I made a note to get the meeting details so I could attend. There was no better time than the present to jump in with both feet.

I spent the rest of the morning and part of the afternoon identifying who managed each product team and reaching out to them individually to get time on their calendars. I was glad Cheryl gave us until Tuesday before our rough drafts were due because I learned quickly that their time was limited. It took some finagling, but I managed to grab an hour tomorrow with the exercise science team, two on Friday, and last but not least, the CBD team Monday morning. That didn't leave me with much time to get my presentation together, but I figured it would have to do.

At 2:30 p.m., I got an alert that the CBD meeting started at three, so I decided to head down for coffee.

I swung by Delaney's office to see if she wanted to go with me, but she wasn't there, so I quickly moved on, not wanting to catch Wayne's attention and risk him accompanying me. As it was, he seemed to be lurking every time I emerged from my office. Once, he even followed me to the restroom, talking the entire time like it was a normal activity. I was merely grateful he hadn't followed me inside, although I was worried for a second that he might.

Since six flights of stairs seemed a bit of overkill right before a meeting, the elevator was my only way down, so there was still a chance I'd encounter him along the way, but I'd have to risk it since I needed caffeine in a bad way. With my fingers crossed, I made my way to the coffee shop in the atrium and stood in line with everyone else looking for their three o'clock pick-me-up. I watched the first few people move through, and I tried to gauge how long it would take. More specifically, whether I should abandon ship to ensure I wasn't late for the meeting.

I waffled back and forth but finally decided the caffeine was necessary to make it through the next couple of hours. I'd learned that meetings tended to make me groggy, and since my calendar seemed to be filling up with them, I had to resort to drastic measures.

When it dwindled to only one person in front of me before it was my turn, a man stepped in front of us. He didn't say excuse me or anything; he merely moved to the counter and told the barista he'd take his usual, whatever that was.

I waited for the woman in front of me to speak up and call him out for cutting the line. She didn't, and when I peeked around her, I noticed she was on the phone, a set of AirPods sticking out of her ears.

Usually, I could let things like this slide, but there were at least eight people behind me, and this guy's disrespect for others was abhorrent. At the very least, he deserved to be called out.

"Excuse me?" I said, prepared to tell him he had to wait with everyone else. "I'm not sure *how* but I don't think you noticed the line."

The words were barely out when he peered back at me, a smirk on his nearly perfect lips. It was then I recognized him from the research I'd done on the company. The inconsiderate stranger was none other than Garrison Walker, the only VP at Primal Instincts that I had yet to meet.

Hello, foot, welcome to mouth.

"And whatever the lady's havin'," he drawled to the woman at the counter as he waved me forward.

I remained firmly planted in place, but then the woman in front of me moved to the side and cast a brief smile my way, leaving me with no choice but to step forward. I did, but I didn't bother to hide my sigh of frustration.

Garrison's eyebrows raised toward his hairline as though silently encouraging me to speak up.

I stared at him, still in shock that he could both be rude and run a company of this size while *being* rude.

Without looking away, I told the woman, "Small cappuccino, extra foam. With two pumps of sugar-free vanilla."

"Strong yet sweet," Garrison said with a lift of his eyebrows. "I like that in a woman."

Do not be charmed by the southern twang or that wicked smile. Do not. Do not. Do not.

Swallowing, I forced a smile. "Not as sweet as you might think."

Something sinful and hot flashed in his blue-gray eyes. "Even better."

Garrison turned to the woman and rapped the counter with his knuckles. "Thank you, darlin'."

Oh, man. He was rude; he should *not* be allowed to sound so … so … sexy.

Garrison motioned for me to move toward the end, where the drinks were served. He didn't pay, but based on the fact she moved on to the next customer, he wasn't required to. I wondered whether the coffee was also free, like the cafeteria food, or if it was merely an executive management perk. I had yet to come here alone, so I didn't know.

Once we reached the end, he turned to me and held out his hand. "Garrison Walker."

"Journey Zeplyn," I said politely, although I would've preferred to lie to him about who I was. That way, he couldn't laugh about me later when he was telling his friends about the oblivious blond girl who had yelled at him in the coffee line.

"Pleasure."

"You realize you cut the line."

His smile was slow and intensely sexy as his gaze swept my face. I took it to mean not many people called him to the carpet very often.

"I have a good reason."

While I should probably be intimidated by the fact he was a VP and could likely determine my fate with the company, I figured since my track record with two others hadn't involved proper manners, there was no reason to start now.

I stared at him, waiting because I could. "I'd love to hear it."

He chuckled, a dark rumble that caused my insides to tingle.

I read that three of them went to the same college, so maybe they took a class on how to make a woman swoon. It seemed to be second nature for them.

Still waiting for him to enlighten me, I took stock of his face and its extraordinary symmetry. Garrison Walker was handsome in a traditional sense: perfectly spaced eyes, patrician nose, sharp jawline, broad forehead. His eyebrows were angled and neatly groomed, his hair was thick and dark and cut business short. He was tall, probably an inch or two over six feet. His suit was tailored to fit his trim, muscular body. He didn't have the bad boy vibe that Hawk did, nor did he have the professional charisma and overwhelming presence that Creed had. Still, there was something ridiculously intriguing about him.

However, I refused to be swept off my feet. It was bad enough when I found myself out of sorts because of Creed, then when Hawk seduced me with his humor and charm. I would not let it happen again. Nope. I had enough material for my fantasies for the foreseeable future; thank you very much.

"Garrison," the man behind the counter called as he pushed two to-go cups toward him.

"Thanks."

He turned and grabbed the cups, and it was then I realized five people were still waiting while we'd been served first.

"This is my reason," he said, passing one of the cups my way. "This way, you won't be late for your next meetin'."

"And how do you know I have a meeting?"

"Because I'm leadin' it." He gestured for me to walk and fell into step with me.

He was close enough that I could smell him. The potent combination of leather and musk went right to my head and warmed the blood in my veins.

Oh, brother. Resist his charms. Don't be drawn in by his pheromones.

"You're leading the meeting?"

"I am."

The meeting was to discuss the CBD product line that would be rolled out this summer. I assumed the marketing department would lead it. From what I read, that was Nick's area, not Garrison's.

"I know what you're thinkin'."

I smiled. "I doubt that."

"You're thinkin' that, accordin' to the company bio, I'm not in marketing."

"How'd—" I stopped walking and turned to face him, canting my head to the side. "Hawk told you about our lunch conversation."

"Guilty." His smile amped up a few megawatts. "In his defense, he tells me a lotta things. Especially when he's smitten."

"Is he smitten often?"

A knowing gleam appeared in his eyes. "Not like this, no."

That admission made my cheeks warm, and a giddy feeling washed over me. I wasn't sure whether it was true, but I thought Hawk and I had shared some pleasant conversations.

"That bother you, darlin'?" he asked, grinning. "That he's taken with you?"

I liked his smile far more than I should. And his voice. And his drawl.

"Say you're right," I prompted. "You thought you'd get my attention so you could vet me?"

"I'm not nearly so chivalrous." He motioned for me to walk again, so I did. "I came to do some recon. See what all the hubbub is about."

"And?"

"Creed and Hawk have damn good taste."

My eyebrows slowly drifted upward. I couldn't tell if he was joking or merely charming me. Either way, I was flattered, but I figured it was time to change the subject.

"So if you're not in marketing, what do you do?"

"VP of Product Development. Although, that's just a fancy title they slapped me with. I'm a biochemical engineer."

I nearly stumbled at the admission but managed to keep my feet under me.

"You're impressed, I know."

From some, that would've sounded like narcissism, but there was something in his tone that lacked egotism. In other words, he was full of charm but unequivocally humble.

"I am, actually."

This time his smile was shy.

"It's rather impressive," I added.

"I was thinkin' the same thing about marketing."

"*No one* thinks that about marketing." I chuckled and waved a dismissive hand. "However, I also have a degree in psychology, so be careful. I might get in your head."

"Beauty *and* brains, a delectable combination."

I could feel my resistance faltering. Oh, who was I kidding? It faltered when he flashed that devious grin.

"Did you meet Creed and Hawk at charm school?"

He didn't miss a beat. "We did, in fact. I was the only one who graduated."

I was laughing as he guided me into one of the larger conference rooms in the heart of the main building, his hand shifting to my lower back. Warmth filled my insides as I realized I liked his easy-going nature.

Someone cleared their throat, and I looked over to see Creed sitting at the back of the room, his eyes locked on us. Only then did I realize the entire room was filled, and all eyes seemed to be pointed at Garrison and me. At least two dozen, all scattered in chairs that had been set up in rows facing the front of the room.

"Thanks for lettin' me cut the line," Garrison said softly near my ear. "If you ever want the lowdown on either of them, let me know. I've got some stories you might like."

I didn't have time to respond because he winked and headed toward the front of the room.

Like yesterday, when Creed found Hawk and me having lunch in the cafeteria, I felt a hint of jealousy coming from him. It made me feel guilty, although I had no idea why. I mean, seriously, we'd had one conversation, which was little more than pleasantries. If he'd wanted to ask me out, he could have. After all, Hawk didn't hesitate to ask me to have coffee with him.

Creed cleared his throat again, and when I tore my gaze away from Garrison, I found him motioning for me to take a seat in the chair beside him. To be fair, it was more of a silent command since he was pointing one big finger at the chair and cocking one of those dark eyebrows at me.

Instantly, I looked for another empty seat only to realize there were none to be had.

With a deep breath in, I moved toward him, pretending not to notice the thunderclouds brewing in his eyes as he tracked me like a predator does its prey.

I might have leaned in just a little as I was taking my seat to see if I could get a whiff of him.

Oh, boy.

Not only did Creed Granger look like a million bucks, he smelled like it too. It was a woody, fresh fragrance with a hint of mandarin, musk, and sandalwood. It smelled … well, on him, it smelled oddly powerful and expensive. Whatever it was suited him very nicely.

Too nicely.

I got settled in my chair, crossed my legs at the knee, and did my best not to touch him with my shoulder. Not an easy feat considering he was so close, and he was so freaking broad; I wasn't sure how he didn't look odd in the regular-sized chair.

As soon as I stopped moving, he leaned over. I was expecting him to comment, but he didn't.

Nope.

He did something else.

The man sniffed me.

"What are you doing?" I whispered.

"Returning the favor," he said in that sinful voice.

I swallowed hard, hating that he caught me smelling him.

"Jasmine and a hint of sandalwood."

My gaze shot to his face, and I was tempted to ask him how he knew that.

He responded with a crooked grin that had me squeezing my legs together. How this man could turn me on with just a smile, I had no freaking idea.

I focused my attention on the front of the room when Garrison began speaking. He only got two sentences in when the rear door of the room opened, and Hawk walked in. Then again, I wasn't sure the way he moved could be described as walking. It was more of a strut, but it didn't seem overdone or meant to garner attention. He merely made a statement with his movements, and I wasn't the only one in the room who couldn't take their eyes off him. I saw Delaney a few seats up, craning her neck to watch him stroll by.

My gaze darted to Hawk. His eyes slid over every person before they seemed to stop on me. Or maybe Creed.

No. Definitely me.

He glanced at Garrison and nodded before moving toward me, although there wasn't a single empty chair. He solved that problem by leaning down and speaking to the man sitting on my other side. A second later, the man in the dress shirt and tie got up and strolled out. Hawk took a seat, inching his chair a little closer to me, although I think I was the only one who noticed.

Scratch that.

Creed noticed.

"Would you like to smell him, too?" Creed whispered directly in my ear.

Chills danced down my spine, and my nipples hardened instantly. I ignored my body's absurd reaction and turned to respond. He leaned toward me so I could speak directly in his ear.

"I already know what he smells like."

I didn't bother telling him Hawk smelled like tobacco and vanilla, a combination I never imagined I would find appealing.

Creed pulled back and met my gaze. I held his stare, refusing to back down from this battle of wills. I wasn't sure what was going on here, but I wouldn't deny that I was fascinated by this man. Completely intrigued.

12

Creed

JOURNEY WAS GOING TO BE THE DEATH of me.

I couldn't pinpoint what it was about the woman that had me wound so tight, but from the moment I saw her in that damn orientation, I hadn't been able to focus for shit. It had been two days, and I'd been practically useless in all aspects of my life, thanks to her. The only plus was that I'd been too busy to seek her out. Otherwise, I'd be doubly screwed.

At the same time, I got the feeling I'd remain that way until I spent time with her. And I didn't mean sitting beside her while Garrison droned on about the benefits of CBD and the various oils and gummies his team was working on. Sure, I was fascinated by what he was doing, but we'd talked about creating this particular product line for years, and now that it was finally coming to fruition, I didn't care anymore. Not about the nuts and bolts of it, anyway.

No, I was only in this room because I saw the invite was rolled out to Cheryl's product marketing managers, and I knew it was an opportunity I couldn't pass up. Clearly, Hawk noticed the same thing since he was present and accounted for. The man went so far as to kick one of our Directors out of the room so he could sit beside Journey. Perhaps having Garrison punish him wasn't the right course of action because it was having no impact on his behavior.

"We've got a few minutes left," Garrison said when the meeting was nearing the end. "Any questions?"

Several hands raised, and I listened with half an ear because I was so caught up in the scent of jasmine and sandalwood. I didn't think anyone else would even notice it, but her unique perfume was now burned into my brain, and every time I inhaled, I smelled her. Already I was addicted, craving something I shouldn't want for many reasons, a couple off the top of my head: One, she worked for me. And for another, she wouldn't last a minute in my world. I had no business—

"I think that's a question better suited for Creed."

With my thoughts effectively interrupted by the mention of my name, I mentally rewound a few seconds and processed what had been said. It was a skill I'd adapted over the years as I'd learned to multitask.

I got to my feet, reluctantly leaving Journey behind as I moved to the front and answered the question regarding whether or not we'd be looking to expand the new CBD line in the future. I gave them my canned response—depending on initial sales and interest, blah, blah, blah. My answer spurred a few more questions, and I addressed each in turn while continuing to look to the back of the room. Each time I did, I found Journey watching me intently, as though she was hanging on my every word. Her interest didn't help this overwhelming obsession I'd formed for her. I couldn't remember the last time I wanted something this badly. Not since I decided to build an empire that would directly support my lifestyle. That decision changed my life. Very much the way Journey had seven years ago when I first laid eyes on her.

I turned the meeting back over to Garrison, but he concluded it before I could reach my seat. I got caught by a couple of people who had questions about profit potential and whatnot. I was answering them when I saw Hawk escorting Journey out of the conference room. But before she disappeared around the corner, her eyes met mine once more.

Yeah. I'd have to do something about this distraction.

Soon.

After the meeting, I returned to my desk to finish up for the day. I managed to have Duke reschedule the five o'clock call on my calendar, telling him I had something I needed to take care of. He didn't ask for details, nor would I have given him any. That was why I liked Duke. He respected the chain of command, both inside and outside the club. He didn't ask; he just did.

I had every intention of going to Journey's office to talk to her, but I quickly redirected across the sixth floor when I saw her talking to Cheryl, Garrison, Hawk, and a couple of other employees. They were laughing at something Garrison said, and I figured it was best not to approach. I had no excuse for being there and wasn't up for talking details and rollout right now. Although, if I had to make a wager, I'd say Garrison and Hawk weren't there to discuss that either.

I hated the disappointment I felt, but I didn't dwell on it. It was probably for the best. As I said, I had no business letting my obsession with her cloud my judgment.

I considered going to the gym to work off some excess energy but went home instead. I could just as easily preoccupy myself by cooking. Since I preferred to do it alone, opportunities were rare. That was what happened when you lived with friends who didn't understand boundaries.

I didn't think any of us ever questioned how we came to live together. It started back when Nick first introduced me to Garrison. I'd been living in a spare storage room at Ray's Gym, where I'd been training at the time. Nick and Garrison lived on campus at Texas A&M, where they both attended classes. We'd known each other for about a year and had started entertaining the idea of starting a gym of our own. It had been a wild-eyed dream, one based on hope and prayers since I was an uneducated orphan making money through unsanctioned fights while they were living on student loans and what they could rake in when they bet on me.

Eventually, we scraped together enough money to get a one-bedroom apartment off-campus and crammed three beds into one room to make it work. It hadn't been easy, but it saved us a shit ton of money. We soon learned that living together allowed us to collaborate more often, our ideas coalescing faster because of our closeness. When we moved to California, living together had become the norm. We were still broke as shit, but we managed to make it work. Even as we began making money, our living situation didn't change, even though the square footage increased over time in the various rentals we occupied. So when I bought this house, it'd been a foregone conclusion that they would reside here. The house was big enough that I didn't have to see them if I didn't want to. Plus, this way, the extra bedrooms didn't go to waste.

The only one who was no longer in residence was Nick. Shortly after he married Kim, he bought a house so they could have more privacy. Admittedly, I was not heartbroken to see her go. I knew Garrison and Hawk weren't either. Our lifestyle wasn't conducive to having a vanilla woman in our house. As for why Nick thought he could subdue his true nature and try out a world without kink, I'd never know. But it didn't surprise me one fucking bit that it didn't work out.

As for my roommates, I enjoyed having them there. They contributed financially as though their names were on the mortgage. Most nights, we'd have dinner, alternating between who bought food or cooked. We worked out at the same gym, usually at the same time. We caught movies or sports games as a group, and we could still manage to wrangle Nick along, thanks to his newly updated relationship status.

As for the house, I had splurged on it the same way I did for my vehicles. I stopped pinching pennies after I made my first billion—a feat that an orphan from Oklahoma never imagined. With its top-end designer touches, the house was the ultimate bachelor pad, built for entertaining. The exterior walls overlooking the city opened to let the outside in, and between the miles of decking and the pool, the hot tubs, the media room, and the game room, there was more than enough to do. But it was the kitchen I liked the most. I'd had it redone before I moved in, designing it myself with commercial-grade appliances for those rare instances when I could relax and do my own thing.

As soon as I got home, I changed into sweats and a T-shirt, then started my prep in the kitchen. Coming up with a recipe using the ingredients in the refrigerator, I got to work. And just as I expected, by the time I was finished, I heard the front door open. A second later, Hawk was walking into the kitchen, nose in the air like a dog sniffing for a treat.

"That girl's got you *all* worked up, huh?" he said, dropping onto one of the stools at the center island.

"You're one to talk."

His smile was mildly disturbing. "Don't think I didn't see you swing through the sixth floor on your way out. And don't tell me you were gonna chat it up with Cheryl," he tacked on. "I'm not an idiot."

"You *are* an idiot," I countered without heat.

"Well, this idiot has her phone number."

"Whose? Cheryl's?"

"Ornery today, are you?" Hawk chuckled. "I've got Journey's number."

"I know." Last night I caught him staring at his phone like a love-struck teenager. I figured he was texting her.

I happened to have her phone number, too, but since I got it through back channels, I didn't mention it. It was also the reason I hadn't called her yet. I'd wanted to, trust me. But I'd never stalked a woman in my life, and I damn sure didn't intend to start now.

Hawk barked a laugh that drew my attention.

"What?"

"You had Duke dig up dirt on her."

"There's no dirt," I assured him, and it was then I realized I had unwillingly copped to what I'd done.

However, Hawk was wrong about one thing. I didn't have Duke dig up anything. I'd done that on my own, plus I relied on the insight I already had because of my relationship with her fathers. Not that I cared to remind Hawk of that. It was enough that I didn't feel guilty pursuing her. I was sure I should, but I didn't.

"None? At all?" Hawk didn't appear convinced.

I jerked my chin in the direction of his phone. "You've got her number. Call her and ask her yourself."

"Are you giving me permission?"

If I thought for one second he gave a shit, I would tell him no. But since I knew he'd do it regardless, it was futile to make a big deal out of it. My hope was that Hawk would lose interest and move on before this became a real issue between us.

Hawk's eyes narrowed. "You think I won't."

The opposite, actually. I thought he would. And since he had a way of communicating with Journey that didn't come across as creepy and stalkerish, I figured that was exactly what he'd do, so I didn't push the issue.

"We had coffee this morning," he said.

That admission had me pausing, a response that gave me away and irked the shit out of me.

Rather than reveal that I was bothered by the fact he'd now had two dates with her, I snorted, then, to change the subject, asked, "Don't you have a date tonight?"

Hawk rested his forearms on the counter. "I canceled it."

I didn't mean to react abruptly, but my gaze slammed into his face. Not once in all the years I'd known Hawk had he ever canceled a date. He might be terminally late to everything, but one thing Hawk did was follow through on his commitments.

Sighing, I grabbed the silicone mitt and moved to pull the tortilla shells out of the oven. "You like her."

There was only sincerity and undeniable respect in his tone when he replied, "Yeah. I like her."

I nodded as I considered what that meant.

While I'd encountered my fair share of obstacles in my path, they didn't happen all that often. At least not since I overcame my shitty childhood. So when I met a woman who captured my attention in a way that didn't even make sense, it was only fitting that one of my best friends decided to get serious about her. More so that it was Hawk, considering our history with one another.

Perhaps I could accept that he was into her, but I knew myself. What I felt in that single moment seven years ago had multiplied tenfold since her arrival in my life. I couldn't ignore that.

Hawk tapped the countertop with his cell phone. "You know, when you finally make your move, she won't want anything to do with me."

He was wrong. Hawk didn't give himself nearly enough credit. He was the whole package, although he rarely let anyone see all sides of himself. Most knew Hawk as the recalcitrant hothead who'd taken the MMA world by storm and then abandoned ship. What most didn't know was that Hawk had two choices: keep fighting and die or retire. Hawk's PR team had played down his injury in the media, but the doctors hadn't pulled any punches when they told him the spinal CSF leak could ultimately lead to death if he didn't stop getting pounded on. Thankfully, the guy was as smart as he was lethal. He chose to live.

"I guess you should enjoy her company while you can," I told him.

His grin was smug. "I think I'll start by texting her."

Fucker.

13

Garrison Walker

"TELL ME HAWK DIDN'T EAT EVERYTHING," I said to Creed when I walked into the house to find him washing dishes.

The kitchen smelled like ground beef and freshly baked something or other. The only time it ever smelled like anything other than the lemon cleaner the housekeeping crew used was when Creed cooked, so I hoped that meant I wouldn't be eating out tonight. I had no idea what was on the menu, but it didn't matter. Creed was a master in the kitchen, and I couldn't remember the last time he'd made anything I didn't like.

Creed jerked his chin in the direction of the refrigerator. "I made you a plate."

"Have I told you how much I love you," I drawled as I strolled across the kitchen, sidestepping the eight-foot-long granite island that separated the appliances from a small seating area that made absolutely no sense to me. It was likely meant to be a breakfast nook, but the designer we'd hired to outfit the house had opted to do something absurd. Then again, the island seated five comfortably, and there was a formal dining room behind the wall of appliances and another on the outdoor patio. Perhaps he thought it would've been overkill to toss in another table and more chairs. I wasn't a designer. I had no fucking clue.

"Ah, hell," I said with a grin as I pulled the taco salad out. "I was kiddin' before, but I think I really do love you."

"Say it again, and you'll make it weird," he retorted.

I grabbed the jar of jalapeño ranch dressing that Creed made from his secret recipe and carried both to the island. Creed supplied me with a fork, sliding it across the granite countertop.

"Thanks. Where's Hawk?"

"Tormenting Journey."

I frowned, pausing mid-pour as I waited for the punchline.

Creed glanced at me over his shoulder. "He's texting her like they're in high school."

I chuckled, then drenched the lettuce and ground beef concoction with dressing. "You know that's how the kids are doin' it these days."

Creed snorted. Hawk was usually the one to give us shit about our ages since we both had nearly a decade on him. Hawk was also the one who was threatening to throw me a fucking over-the-hill party when I turned forty in March. I promised to throw him *down* the hill if he followed through.

I screwed the lid back on the mason jar and set it aside. "You linin' up more punishment for later?"

"No." Creed turned off the water and grabbed a dish towel. He turned around to face me as he leaned against the counter. "It's what he wants."

I shoveled a forkful of salad into my mouth to avoid telling him I wasn't so sure that was Hawk's only motivation. After all, I'd seen firsthand Hawk's interactions with her this afternoon. I'd only been teasing Journey earlier when I told her Hawk was smitten, but I hadn't been wrong. What I hadn't realized was that Journey was equally as taken with him as he was with her.

"What aren't you telling me, G?"

I shook my head, took another bite.

The last thing I wanted to do was get in the middle of this ménage à trois or incite Creed somehow. His relationship with Hawk was a point of contention, one I'd inadvertently been dragged into when they'd had their falling out. In all fairness, I had warned Hawk that one day he would push Creed too far. Then the fool gave Creed an ultimatum, declaring he wanted more from their relationship. The problem was, Hawk had been the only one of them who'd seen it as a relationship. Aside from the friendships he'd established with the three of us, Creed didn't do relationships. Hell, I wasn't even sure he was capable.

Which was why I found his interest in Journey so fascinating. Not once in the nearly twenty years that I'd known the man had he ever laid claim to anyone, yet that seemed to be what he was doing with Journey.

"Why're you interested in her, anyway?" I prompted, continuing to eat so he couldn't grill me for answers. "I mean, aside from the fact she's gorgeous."

And she was, but she was also young and sweet and … the exact opposite of any woman Creed had ever shown even a modicum of interest in. Not to mention, the only thing more vanilla than her was the orchid that vanilla beans came from.

"I don't know."

I swallowed and choked on a mouthful of cheddar cheese and lettuce. I'd been expecting some sort of denial or, at the most, an admission that he wanted to dominate her. That would've been far more Creed-like than *I don't know.*

Clearly sensing I was dangerously close to choking to death, Creed grabbed a beer from the fridge and slid it toward me before taking one for himself.

I twisted off the top, flipped it at him, and took a long pull. It took three times to clear my throat.

I stared at him as my throat muscles settled. I skimmed my memory bank to see if I ever recalled him even mentioning her in all the time I'd known him. I couldn't. Hell, I couldn't even remember her parents mentioning her, and I'd talked to Roman, Ryder, and Cadence on plenty of occasions during their tenure at Primal.

"You didn't meet her for the first time this week, did you?"

"Meet her? Yes," he said, tossing the dish towel on the counter. "See her? No."

I nodded with my chin, urging him to continue.

"Seven years ago. At Cadence's fortieth birthday party," he explained. "She was there that night. I got a glimpse of her, but we weren't introduced."

A glimpse? The fiercest Primal Dom I'd ever met had been bowled over by a glimpse? What the hell was this world coming to?

"You've been hangin' onto this crush for seven years?"

He cast that look that said, *what the fuck do you think?* It didn't answer a damn thing, but it was enough for me to know I should back off.

"And it's not a fucking crush," he grumbled.

I grinned behind the lip of my beer bottle. *There* was the Creed I knew.

I took a swallow, set the bottle down, and picked up my fork. I poked at my food, trying to decide how I wanted to tell him the cold, hard truth.

"What?" Creed snapped. "Just fucking spit it out already."

I met his gaze. "I know you're givin' him some rope to hang himself, but you should know it's not a one-sided attraction."

Creed's chin lifted, his eyes boring holes in my face. I could practically see the wheels turning in his head, but he wasn't about to give anything away.

I finished the rest of my food while Creed mulled over that information.

"I know you don't want my advice," I told him as I took my plate to the sink. "But that girl … she's somethin'. She might be single right now, but I can't imagine that'll last too much longer."

Not if Hawk had a say in it, at least.

"And what do you propose I do about that?"

I glanced over my shoulder. "Maybe try puttin' in some effort."

"Yeah," Creed acknowledged, but I could tell by his tone that he was still lost somewhere in his head.

If nothing else, this was going to get interesting.

14

Journey

WHEN I LEFT THE OFFICE THIS EVENING, I promised myself I would stop fantasizing about a man I had no business fantasizing about.

I failed.

Epically.

And I had hard proof, thanks to the short story I posted an hour ago.

For some reason, I couldn't stop coming up with wildly erotic scenarios that involved sexy men in powerful positions, each one more inappropriate than the last. I hadn't intended to do it, but when I got to my parents' house, I'd been compelled to sit down and write. Within seconds, a quick and dirty fantasy came out about a sinful cowboy doing filthy things to me in a shadowy corner while everyone else focused on the presenter at the front of the room. Well, everyone except the two men who couldn't seem to take their eyes off us.

Yep. Garrison Walker was the focus of my last erotic fairy tale, and Creed and Hawk were the onlookers.

What was worse? Well, that would be Rhylee calling me out on it. I had no idea she even paid attention to my posts, but ten minutes after I put it up, she texted me.

💬 IS THIS YOU EXPLORING YOUR EXHIBITIONIST SIDE?

I'd stared at the text for at least ten minutes before I managed to come up with a reply.

> I'VE BEEN READING A NEW BOOK SERIES. IT PROVIDED SOME INSPIRATION.

Whether she believed me or she was simply too busy to push for more details, I wasn't sure, but Rhylee hadn't messaged me back. However, her question had spurred some questions of my own. Was I an exhibitionist? Was I interested in an erotic encounter with more than one person? Or was I simply trying to work out the attraction I had for three different men?

While I should probably question where these new revelations belonged in what I considered my ideal relationship, I'd decided it wasn't necessary. Not yet. It wasn't like I was in a position where it mattered whether I had to choose one man over another, so it would've been a waste of time. No matter how much I thought about Creed, he had yet to make a move, and I was starting to think he had no intention of doing so. As for Garrison … well, I thought there might be something there, but it wasn't of the romantic variety. Aside from some light flirting, I didn't get the feeling Garrison was looking for anything more than friendship, and I was okay with that.

On the flip side, there was one sexy man who was effectively distracting me. With each interaction, I found myself more and more intrigued by Hawk. He was funny and smart and sexy as hell. I liked that I could talk to him without feeling awkward. The back-and-forth text exchange that'd been going on for the better part of the last two hours had been lively and fun, making me smile and laugh. Who didn't want someone who knew how to make them laugh? Hawk was adding fuel to the fire because he had a wicked sense of humor, and he knew just what to say to get me hot and bothered, although I wasn't even sure he realized he was.

Which was the reason I was heading for the shower, my trusty vibrator in my hand.

If I were at my apartment, I wouldn't need the vibrator because I could use the fancy shower sprayer I'd bought. However, at my parents' house, the shower in my private bathroom didn't have one, which was why I had packed Buzz. Yep, that was what I called it because even a slender, purple vibrator deserved a name. Not that I talked to my vibrator, nor did I moan his name when he got the job done.

I set Buzz on the niche in the tile and turned on the water. It was instant-hot, but I liked the steam it built when it ran for a minute, so I stripped off my clothes and brushed my hair. By the time I was done, the air was thick and warm, filtering up and over the glass enclosure.

As soon as I stepped inside, closing the door behind me, I found myself smiling. More so when I closed my eyes, tilted my head back, and let the water beat down on my head. I let it soak my hair, and I didn't fight the mental image of Creed that formed in my mind's eye. Why I was fantasizing about him when I'd been thinking about Hawk, I couldn't explain. For whatever reason, he seemed to be at the heart of my arousal. Ever since I heard his voice that first time, I couldn't help imagining all the dirty, filthy things he might say to me. It was probably wrong to think of him that way, but I couldn't help it, and I didn't want to. I found Creed Granger sinfully delicious, and where was the harm in having dirty thoughts about the man? It wasn't like I would act on them.

Well, I didn't think I would.

Okay, that was a lie. Given half a chance, I'd crawl all over him like a jungle gym.

I ran through my nightly ritual. Shampoo, conditioner, body wash. Since I was wearing a skirt tomorrow, I took the time to shave my legs. While I was at it, I also touched up the other pertinent parts. By the time I was finished, I was relaxed from the heat of the water and the sinful thoughts flitting around inside my head.

As I reached for Buzz, my cell phone rang from the other room. It was probably my mother calling to check up on the cats. Just thinking it might be her was enough to pull me right out of my fantasy and back to reality.

"Sorry, Buzz," I said as I turned off the water. "Maybe later."

It was then I realized maybe I did talk to my vibrator.

Ten minutes later, after I'd dried off, twisted my hair up in a towel on top of my head, and lathered my entire body with lotion, I emerged from the bathroom to check my phone. I was right. It was my mother.

I pulled on a robe, then dialed her back as I headed downstairs to grab a glass of water.

"What's up, Mom-er-ific?"

I could hear the smile in her voice when she said, "I thought maybe you were in bed already."

"Not yet, but I'm heading that way."

"How are my babies?"

Her *babies* came strolling into the kitchen, staring up at me with hopeful yet calculating eyes.

"They're rotten as ever." I pulled open the refrigerator. "But you already knew that."

"I did, yes. And how was your day?"

"Good." I told her some high-level stuff that happened, including the pseudo-competition I was in with my co-workers.

"So, which do you want to do?"

"I don't know yet," I admitted. "I want to do my due diligence."

"Well, honey, you'll shine no matter where your heart leads you."

The woman always knew exactly what to say. She was never without some words of encouragement.

"Now, tell me about your co-workers."

"We're a small team, only four of us and my manager. Delaney's the feisty one," I said with a smile. "She's upbeat, always teasing and laughing. Then there's Gem. I haven't quite figured them out yet, but I think we'll get along fine. And my manager Cheryl is awesome. She's very encouraging."

"You said there are four of you plus your manager. Who's the fourth?"

"His name's Wayne. He's a new hire like me." That was all I told her because anything more wouldn't have been nice.

"Are you having issues with him?"

"I'm not sure I'd call them issues, but he's ... not a very nice man."

"Older? Younger?"

I took a glass out of the cabinet. "Does it matter?"

"No, of course not. But since you're all clammed up, I must drag the details out of you somehow."

I laughed. "He's not worth talking about, I assure you."

"Meet anyone else since you started? On other teams?"

My thoughts immediately jumped to my encounter with Garrison at the coffee shop. Self-preservation kept me from sharing that tale with her. I was already infatuated with two men. Three would make it ... complicated.

"Lots of people," I said instead. "There's a guy named Gregorio who works in product development."

There was a hint of excitement in her voice. "Is he Italian?"

I opened the freezer to grab a few ice cubes and dropped them into my glass. "He is," I drawled in an effort to taunt her.

"Is he hot?"

"Not even a little," I said with a small laugh.

"You're such a tease."

I pulled the water pitcher out of the refrigerator. "I learned that from Obi-Wan and Chewbacca." My dads were notorious for their jokes.

"But it's good? Work, I mean?"

"Yup. I'm getting the hang of it." I filled my glass, set the pitcher down, and hopped up on the counter. The cats were instantly there, twining around me like living, breathing feather boas. "Have y'all made it to your turnaround point yet?"

"Sometime tomorrow, they tell me." She sighed. "I'm not sure how we'll be able to make these trips more than once a year if they want to stop at every truck stop along the way."

I had a sneaking suspicion *truck stop* was a euphemism for where they were really going. My parents didn't think I knew that they were into BDSM, but I'd known for more years than I cared to admit. Sure, they were discreet about it—thank God—but like I said, I was nosy, and sometimes I found out things that were better left as secret.

"As long as they're getting me shot glasses from every state, tell them they can stop as often as they like."

"I'll be sure to do that."

"Everything else good?" I prompted, wanting to ensure there wasn't something my mother needed to unload. She got a little frantic from time to time and just needed to hash things out, and I happened to be the perfect sounding board. I was sure she was reaching her breaking point because this trip was two solid weeks on the road, living out of a house on wheels. Regardless of how nice it was, she was still confined to one space for days on end.

"Better than good."

"What is it?" I asked because I could tell she was holding something back.

She hesitated before saying, "We might be delayed a little longer than I thought."

"Okay."

"I really wanted—wait. You don't mind?"

"Of course not. Why would I?"

"We're impeding your plans."

I huffed a laugh. "My only plans involve work. And catching up on some reading."

"You're sure?"

"Of course." I looked down at the cats, who were now head-butting my hands whenever I stopped petting them. "Plus, the divas are doing fine. They like me most of the time."

"They like you always."

It was true. They did.

"You don't have to rush back on my account," I told her, ensuring she heard my sincerity. "I've got no problem keeping an eye on them if y'all want to detour somewhere else along the way."

"Okay, good. I'll let you know for sure next week. I love you, honey."

"Love you too, Momster. Tell Obi-Wan and Chewbacca I love them, too."

We said our goodbyes, and the call ended. I hopped down from the counter and gave the cats one final pat each before I snagged the glass of water and headed back upstairs. I made a detour to the bathroom to remove the towel from my hair and ran a comb through it. I considered grabbing Buzz from the shower but decided not to bother when I checked my texts and saw there was another message from Hawk.

💬 YOU THINK MAYBE YOU COULD DO ME A FAVOR?

I sat on the edge of my bed and tapped out a response.

💬 DEPENDS. IF IT REQUIRES ME TO GET DRESSED, THEN PROBABLY NOT.

The three dots signifying he was typing appeared, but they disappeared again, only to return and go away. It was a full minute before I got another message.

💬 ARE YOU SAYING YOU'RE NAKED RIGHT NOW?

💬 WELL, SURE. UNDERNEATH MY CLOTHES, I AM.

I didn't tell him I was only wearing a robe. Where was the fun in that?

The dots started playing hide and seek again, but I beat him to it.

💬 WHAT WAS THE FAVOR YOU NEEDED?

💬 HELL IF I REMEMBER. NOW THE ONLY THING I CAN THINK ABOUT IS YOU NAKED.

"Don't go to sleep in there, Buzz," I called out to my vibrator. "We might be back on for our date."

I decided it wasn't weird to talk to him. It would've been weird if I called his name during orgasm.

Which I didn't. I was positive about that.

I waited a few minutes to see if Hawk was going to respond. When he didn't, I decided to get ready for bed. After plugging my laptop in on my desk, I flipped off the lights in the bedroom and the bathroom, slipped my robe off before ensuring my charging cable was plugged in and my alarm was set on my phone. I was about to place my phone on the magnetic charging mount when it buzzed in my hand. I peered down at the screen. It was another message from Hawk, only this time, there were no words, only what appeared to be a phone number.

💬 WHAT'S THAT?

💬 CREED'S. I THINK HE'S JEALOUS YOU'RE NOT TEXTING HIM.

I was curious why Hawk would think that or how he would know, but I decided not to ask.

💬 WHAT WOULD YOU LIKE ME TO DO WITH THE? IS WRITING IT ON A PUBLIC RESTROOM WALL STILL A THING?

💬 🌀

I stared at the phone for the longest time, waiting for him to say something. All while I was memorizing the ten digits he had provided me. Ten digits that were a direct line to Creed Granger, a man I had no business thinking about when I already had one I was chatting with. Then again, Hawk was the one who gave me the number. If he were worried about me being interested in someone else, he wouldn't have done it, right?

Because I knew I'd never fall asleep if I didn't do something, I pulled up another text message and entered the number.

💬 I GOT THIS FROM A BATHROOM WALL. SAID CALL FOR A GOOD TIME. DOES IT WORK THE SAME WITH TEXT? CAN YOU GIVE A GOOD TIME THROUGH TEXT? OR IS THAT JUST WEIRD?

I hit send, smiling so wide my cheeks hurt. I hurried to add more.

💬 OH, AND YOU MIGHT WANT TO UNFRIEND HAWK ASAP IF YOU VALUE YOUR PRIVACY. THIS IS JOURNEY, BTW.

As I stared at the phone, wondering if he'd message me back, butterflies started rioting in my belly. I had no idea why I was so anxious, but I was. It wasn't a good feeling, either. It was probably one of the reasons I didn't date. I didn't care too much for the overwhelming anticipation that came along with it.

And that right there was a load of crap. The only reason I hadn't dated anyone since high school was that I'd been so overwhelmed by my class schedule. Somewhere along the way, I had convinced myself I'd done it because of my dedication to my future, but the truth was, there'd been no time for anyone or anything except school.

When there was no response from Creed a few minutes later, I sighed.

"Well, I tried," I said aloud as I clicked the button to turn off the screen, then stretched out so I could reach the charging mount.

This time I managed to get my phone hooked up, but as soon as I set it down, it rang.

Not a text. A phone call.

"Oh, shit," I muttered as I sat up, immediately flipping off the lamp. It wasn't a FaceTime call, but my brain didn't process that.

I hit the button to answer, wanting to say something witty and cute, but nothing came out.

"Journey?"

Oh, dear heavens above. *That voice.*

"Are you there?"

"Yep." It came out as a squeak, so I cleared my throat and tried again. "Yeah. I'm here."

Creed was silent for a moment, but I could hear him breathing. It was absurdly sexy to listen to this man breathe while I was naked in a dark room. It went on for what felt like an eternity. When Creed continued to say nothing, I started to feel awkward.

"I didn't mean to freak you out," I told him. "I just wanted to ... uh ... say hello."

"Hello."

I wondered if he had ever considered being a phone sex operator. Women and men alike would spend millions to get off to a voice like his. I know I would've. Buzz would require me to stockpile Duracells.

"What are you wearing?" I asked, purposely teasing him.

Creed huffed a laugh before speaking his first complete sentence. "Did Hawk put you up to that?"

"No." I flopped back onto my bed and forced myself to relax. "I'm only joking. You sound tense. I wanted to make it less weird. Didn't work, huh?"

"Oh, it worked. I'm no longer thinking about how sexy your voice is over the phone," he said smoothly. "Now I'm wondering what you're wearing."

"Nothing," I blurted. "I mean, wait. You think my voice is sexy? Because I was thinking the same about yours. Like … phone sex … I mean … uh … wearing … I sleep naked. *Shit.* Oh, God…"

My face was so red I could feel the flames shooting out of the tips of my ears. I totally screwed *that* up.

"Journey…"

The way he said my name sounded like a warning, and it turned me on. Then again, everything about this man turned me on. Every. Single. Thing.

Neither one of us said a word for a solid minute. At that point, I swore my heart would beat right out of my chest.

"Creed?" I swallowed hard, then forced myself to continue. "I'm going to hang up now."

"Probably a good idea."

"I'm glad you think so."

"I'll see you tomorrow," he added.

"Yeah. Okay." Before I did something I'd never recover from, I hung up.

As I lay there, staring at the dark ceiling, I realized that I was breathing hard and nothing had happened.

Literally nothing.

So why was I hoping nothing would happen again tomorrow?

15

Journey

I spent most of Thursday morning alternating between reviewing the detailed org chart of the entire company, the evacuation plans that notated every floor in the building, and my actual job, which involved doing outside research on products similar to those we were looking to release. Although I would've loved to spend every spare minute trying to determine whether there was a connection between the actual company and the secret sex club, earning a paycheck was more important. This meant if I wanted to keep earning one, I had to tackle the tasks I was assigned and stop looking for the secret passageways that were rumored to be beneath this building.

Granted, it was fun to play the super sleuth. Or it would've been if I wasn't more worried that I'd get caught. I don't think I was cut out for deception. It would've been nice if I'd realized that before I started working here or before I'd gotten my two best friends caught up in this conspiracy with me.

Since I couldn't turn back time, I decided I could focus my efforts on something I *was* good at. After identifying five of our top competitors, I checked out their websites, making note of things that caught my attention, some that I found were irrelevant to the consumer's interest, and jotting everything in my notebook under the heading: Beneficial to my Success.

After that, I spent two hours browsing the Primal Instincts website, focusing primarily on the brand and the things people recognized when they thought of the company. I'd never done a product launch from start to finish before, but I'd engaged in various in-class projects that were very similar to the real thing. I was comfortable with the steps, so I created my checklist, one that was just for me and one I would include in my presentation to Cheryl and the executives.

When lunchtime came around, I ventured down to the cafeteria, figuring I'd grab something to take back to my desk so I could keep working before my afternoon meeting with the Reflect team. As I was making my way through the dining room, I noticed Hawk, Garrison, and Nick sitting at a table in the corner. Nick's back was to me, but I could see Garrison's profile and Hawk's sinful smirk. Without thinking, I smiled when Hawk looked up, his gaze moving with me.

Although I was tempted to detour to say hello, I remained focused and headed for the food prep area to find something to eat that wouldn't bog me down for the afternoon. While standing in line for sub sandwiches, I saw Gem and Delaney talking animatedly by the wall of refrigerators. They were too far away for me to make out what they were saying, but it looked heated.

When it was my turn to order, I stepped up to the counter, rattled off my request, and then moved down the line as they prepared my food. At the end, I took my paper-wrapped sandwich, then headed over to get a bottle of water.

"I saw her," Gem declared. "She was having coffee with Jacob Hawkins yesterday morning."

"Can you blame her? The guy's hot."

"She had lunch with him the day before."

"Since when are you obsessed with Journey's romantic life?"

I swallowed past the lump that formed when I heard my name.

"You don't find that odd?"

"Why would I? If she wants that sexy man to take her to the mat, more power to her. I wouldn't say no to the guy if he asked *me* to have lunch with him."

Gem continued with, "I think she was buttering him up for the product launch selection."

"No way." Delaney waved them off. "You said yesterday morning. What time?"

"I don't know." Gem cast a sardonic look at their naked wrist. "I didn't look at my watch."

"Was it before or after Cheryl's meeting?"

"Before."

She huffed a laugh. "It's a coincidence."

"Then explain what she was doing walking into the meeting yesterday afternoon with Garrison Walker."

Delaney's mouth opened, but nothing came out.

"Yeah. He bought her coffee."

Technically, it was free, I thought to myself.

"Or what about when she was cozied up to Jacob Hawkins *and* Creed Granger *during* the meeting? You think that was a coincidence, too?"

Delaney didn't speak again.

In all fairness, the fictional narrative Gem had created didn't paint me in a good light. They were wrong, of course.

"And if she uses that to get the product launch she wants…?"

Delaney's expression morphed into one of concern. "She wouldn't do that."

"Really? You know her well enough to say she's not vindictive? Tell me you won't be pissed if you end up with the fitness tracker. Seriously. You and I both know that'll be scrapped before the end of the year."

My heart sank in my chest the longer they went on. I never considered anyone noticing that I was talking to Hawk, Creed, or Garrison, much less that they would think I was doing it for my own gain.

Not wanting to hear anything more, I turned the opposite way and slipped out without either noticing. It wasn't until I was at the door leading out of the dining room that I heard someone call my name. I glanced over to see Hawk standing up, waving me over.

Figuring it wouldn't look good if Gem and Delaney caught me talking to any of them right now, I pretended I didn't see him, turning away abruptly and hurrying back to my office as fast as my legs could carry me. Before I got to the sixth floor, my phone buzzed in my pocket. I pulled it out and saw a text from Hawk.

WHAT WAS THAT?

The elevator doors opened. I stepped out, debating whether I should respond. I wanted to, but I wasn't sure I should. And what was I supposed to say? Tell him the truth? That my co-workers thought I was flirting to progress myself in this competition?

Before I could decide what or how to respond, I turned and saw Wayne coming out of my office.

"What are you doing?" I picked up the pace, calling after him as he scurried to his office next door.

He glanced over his shoulder, then disappeared inside, closing the door behind him.

I went into my office and looked around. The notebook on my desk was open to the page I was making notes on earlier. I knew I closed it before I left because I would never leave it open. Some might've called it slight OCD, but I was a stickler for organization, and once I'd completed a task, I reorganized so I would be ready for the next one. Plus, one of my pens was lying on top of it, which I knew I had put back because, yes, I happened to be a little obsessive about that, too.

I stood at my desk and peered down at the notes. It was open to the details of the competitor's products that I was jotting down. I looked up at the wall that was shared between us and frowned. Was he copying my stuff?

"Are you really surprised?" I muttered, dropping into my chair. It did seem like something Wayne would do. He wasn't exactly the type who wanted to put in the effort. At least not based on what little I knew of him.

My phone buzzed again.

💬 ARE YOU IGNORING ME?

> 💬 OF COURSE NOT. I'M PREPARING FOR A MEETING, SO I'M WORKING WHILE I EAT.

He didn't respond, but I shoved it out of my mind just as quickly as I shoved the sandwich aside, no longer hungry.

The afternoon dragged on, although I spent an hour with the Reflect team learning as much as possible about their product. It was a good name for what it was, I figured. The four-foot-tall, wall-mounted machine was a complicated gadget. It was a combination of weight training and video exercise guides. It came complete with personalized workout programs, all displayed on the reflective front, allowing the user to gauge their form while engaged. It was designed for home use, although they were working on a version that could be utilized and implemented in class settings at the Primal Instincts gyms across the country.

I took notes throughout the tour, asking questions as they came to me and adding some ideas I had for later. Their goal for the launch was November, with a plan to start preorders that should deliver by Christmas. That meant there was plenty of time to work out the details.

After that, I returned to my office and transcribed my notes onto my computer to access later. When I was finished, I took one of the follow-up classes from the new-hire orientation, which I dragged out until five o'clock. At that point, I slipped out without saying a word to anyone, not wanting to risk getting the stink eye from Gem or Delaney, who apparently thought I had some sort of agenda that included seducing men to get preferable treatment on a work project. *Who* did that?

The moment I stepped outside, I felt a sense of relief. As though I'd been stifled inside the walls because of what I'd overheard at lunch. Some of the tension drained from my shoulders as I made my way to my car, only for it to return when I noticed a man leaning against it.

"Hey, you want to grab drinks? Talk about the projects?"

"No, Wayne, I don't," I told him as plainly as I possibly could. God knows if I tried for polite, he'd think I was hitting on him.

His gaze slid over me, and I suddenly felt the urge to shower.

"You sure about that?"

"I'm sure."

He stood tall. "All right. Your loss."

"What were you doing in my office?" I asked before he turned to walk away.

"I … uh … needed to borrow a pen."

He was lying. For one, my pens were all there when he left. I guess he could've jotted something down while he was in there. I did have a stack of Post-It notes on the desk. Maybe he took one.

It was a stretch, but since I couldn't prove anything, I decided to give him the benefit of the doubt—at least as far as he believed. "Alright. Next time, ask, please."

His response was a grunt before he openly glared at my chest. There was nothing provocative about the outfit I was wearing, but you wouldn't know it by the way he was trying to melt my sweater with his laser beam gaze.

I refrained from shuddering in disgust, not wanting him to mistake it for something else.

"Good night, Wayne."

I took my time getting into my car, ensuring he walked away. When I was confident he was gone, I started the engine with a sigh. My hand was on the gear shift when someone knocked on my window.

I screamed.

It was weird.

I covered it with a laugh when I looked over to see Hawk standing at my door.

Oh, boy.

This was not what I needed right now. The building was emptying, which meant there was the potential for someone to see us talking.

I turned off the engine, then fumbled to find the button for the window. As it lowered, he bent down, casually resting his arm on the car's roof.

"Hi." I hoped I sounded chipper, but I was confident I failed when Hawk's eyebrows slid lower.

His eyes narrowed. "You okay?"

"Peachy. You?"

He smiled, effectively disarmed. "Better now."

I fought the urge to look around to see if anyone was paying attention to us.

"What's up?" I prompted, not wanting it to get weirder.

"You never did answer me about that dinner date."

I smiled because it was hard not to. There was something about this man. His cool confidence, that panty-melting smile … he disarmed with his charm.

"The one that precedes our trip to Vegas for Elvis nuptials?" I teased, remembering that conversation.

"That'd be the one."

Recalling the gossip between Gem and Delaney, I sighed. "I don't think that's a good idea. My co-workers … they already think I'm seeking favoritism."

"From?"

"You. Creed. Garrison."

His expression sobered. "Is that right?"

I nodded nervously. "Yup." I looked out the front window. "They saw us talking."

"Talking's a crime now. Interesting."

I was so surprised by the curt response that I cut my gaze to him and stared at his handsome face. I couldn't decipher his expression, but I was tempted to say he was pissed. Or hurt. Maybe both.

"I figure it might be best to keep a low profile until after the product marketing managers are decided."

"*That's* what this is about? Shame on you for thinking we could be swayed."

"I didn't think that," I countered quickly. "I—"

I cut myself off when I saw a slow smile form on his mouth.

"I didn't take you for the kind to bow to peer pressure, Journey Zeplyn."

Now *my* eyes narrowed. I was defensive because he made a valid point, not because he was wrong. I'd never been one to give in to pressure. Not from anyone. I'd made a point to blaze my own path, to do my own thing, taking a page right out of my parents' book. I never cared whether I was popular at school—which I wasn't—or whether or not everyone liked me—which they didn't. I took my mother's advice, the piece she harped on for as far back as I could remember: *Put yourself first because when it comes down to it, you're the only one you have to answer to.*

Something about that had always struck me as true, so I went with it. I wasn't sure my mother meant for me to try out for football—although I did, once, but didn't make the team—or for me to campaign for gender-neutral bathrooms during my senior year—although I did and won, thank you very much.

"You eat meat?"

"Only if it's cooked," I answered.

That slow smile returned. "Good. Grab a burger with me. I'll meet you there."

"In-N-Out?" I asked hopefully.

"Sure."

Since I picked the place myself, I didn't have an excuse now.

"Wait here," Hawk instructed, tapping his hand on the edge of the door. "I'll pull around."

I nodded because I wasn't sure what else to say.

When he walked away, I glanced in the side-view mirror to admire how good he looked from behind. The man filled out a pair of jeans like no one I'd ever seen. His shirt hugged his broad shoulders, wide chest, and tapered waist, but the way that denim caressed his impressive backside … yum.

Since Creed and Garrison wore suits, it made me wonder if Hawk enjoyed bucking the system. He seemed like the type who would.

After a few minutes, as I drummed my fingers on the steering wheel, I was beginning to wonder if he had forgotten he was supposed to return when I heard the rumble of a motor. A second later, he appeared behind me, straddling a motorcycle.

Oh, man. His hotness factor just rose a few million degrees.

"Ready?" he called out.

I nodded, although I wasn't sure he could see me. I tapped my horn lightly to confirm, giggling as I did. A second later, he revved his engine, lifted his feet, and rocketed toward the exit. I avoided looking at him as I backed out of the space, fearful I would rear-end someone if I did. He was waiting for me at the parking lot exit, and before I could stop behind him, he propelled his motorcycle forward, careening down the road to the burger place we had agreed on.

When the traffic cleared, I pulled out and followed, my smile now firmly planted on my face. There was a tingling in my belly, almost as though the butterflies that were usually there had been electrified. I liked the feeling.

As soon as I parked my car and turned off the engine, Hawk was at my door, opening it for me. He waited for me to get out, then closed it behind me.

Once we'd ordered and received our food trays, Hawk led the way to a booth tucked into a corner. It wasn't private by any means, but at least it wasn't in the middle of the chaos of families out enjoying their meals.

He gestured for me to sit on the side against the wall, and I did, scooting toward the center. I expected him to sit across from me, but instead, he took his seat on the same side, forcing me to move over a little. He didn't crowd me, but that did nothing to put space between us. He was close enough that every fiber of my being was inherently aware of how good he smelled.

"Are you originally from California?" I blurted, figuring if I didn't stop breathing him in, I might do something I shouldn't.

"Arizona. Sedona," he answered readily, unwrapping his burger. "When I was ten, my dad left, and my mom moved us to Vegas."

"Vegas? Really? No wonder you want to get married there." I laughed when he cut his gaze to me and winked. "I've never been."

"I'll have to take you."

While I ate, I gave myself the freedom to imagine a trip to Vegas with Hawk. The fantasy was filled with laughter and heat, something else he offered me with little effort.

Before it could gain too much momentum, I reined the wandering thought in, fidgeting with a napkin. "Did she move there for work? Your mom?"

"Yep. She's still there. She worked at the Aria until last year. Now she's at the Monolith. She loves it."

I loved the way his voice elevated when he talked about his mother. It sounded like they had a good relationship.

I was hesitant when I asked, "And your dad?"

He chewed, then wiped his mouth. "I've seen him a few times over the years. I thought we might work it out for a while, but then he tried to piggyback on my career. He was pissed when I retired. Told me to man up. I told him to fuck off." His eyes slid toward me, and a sheepish smirk appeared. "Excuse my language."

I grinned because he was too cute.

"I don't hear from him much anymore. And when I do, I'm too skeptical about his intentions. It's easier to keep my distance."

"I'm sorry."

"Don't be." He tugged me against his side and put his arm over my shoulders. "I'm a well-rounded adult. I've got no regrets. Now tell me about your folks. Where are they?"

"Road trip."

The arm he had over my shoulders reached forward, causing me to lean as he stole a French fry.

"And what do they do?"

I stole one of his in return. "My mom's a psychiatrist. She specializes in human sexuality."

"Sounds ... devious."

I laughed. "It's interesting. And she's good at what she does."

"What about your dads?"

I paused as I chewed. I didn't remember telling him I had two dads, but considering how much we had talked, I probably did.

"They ... um..."

I didn't miss the look he sent me, the way his forehead creased. He was probably wondering why I was hesitant.

I took a deep breath and exhaled slowly. "They own their own business. They're ... uh ... stunt coordinators."

"For movies or television?"

I nodded. "Both."

"Anything I might've seen?"

I shrugged. "Depends. Do you like box office hits?"

"It's like pulling teeth." He chuckled, bringing his arm down so he could finish his burger. "I've seen a few in my time."

"Then I'm sure you've seen one of theirs. They're in high demand."

"So you've met some famous people, huh?"

"Comes with the territory."

"And yet you downplay it. Why is that?"

"For me, it's normal. I've never known anything different. Some people don't know how to handle it."

He shifted his body, angling toward me. "I can assure you, I'm not interested in making nice with you to meet your folks."

"Promise?"

"I'd like to meet them one day," he said. "But only because I'd like to get to know my girlfriend's family."

My cheeks warmed from his statement, but I shrugged it off. "That would be interesting. Considering they might be your biggest fans. Next to me, of course."

"You're a fan?"

"Oh, yeah. I could recite your stats to prove it if you'd like."

His grin widened. "Not necessary, smokeshow. I'll take your word for it."

Turned out Jacob Hawkins was a fantastic date.

We spent another hour chatting about nothing of importance, although every word he spoke felt important. We didn't discuss anything related to work, only personal preferences for things like restaurants, movies, and rock bands. I learned that he preferred sushi, while I leaned toward steakhouses. We did agree that burgers could and should be eaten at least five days a week. Hawk was a fan of *Jason Bourne*, while I tended to gravitate toward *Transformers*. And he insisted AC/DC was far better than Aerosmith. I disagreed wholeheartedly, but I didn't tell him as much.

The entire meal was casual, with a lot of laughter and smiles being cast back and forth. I liked the way he listened to me, the way he focused on my every word. I'd never felt quite as important as I did with him. As though everything I said was something he was eager to hear.

After we finished, he led me outside, then took my hand to walk me to my car. The strength in his fingers sent tingles through my entire body. I couldn't remember the last time anyone held my hand.

We were silent as we approached my car, then when Hawk lifted our joined hands and stared at my fingers. He touched them with his other hand as though he was fascinated.

"I … uh…" I smiled shyly, looking down at my feet. "Thank you for dinner."

The edge of his finger tapped under my chin, and I lifted my head, meeting his gaze. He skimmed my face as though he was trying to memorize my features. I couldn't look away, awestruck by how hot he made me with a simple look.

"I had a great time," he said softly, his finger lightly brushing my neck.

I felt it throughout my entire body.

"Journey?"

I couldn't look away. I was lost in his gaze. "Hmm?"

He leaned in, his lips inching closer to mine. I didn't move. I couldn't. The only thing I could think about was this man's lips on mine. Every time I tried to convince myself I was holding out for Creed to make a move, I ended up thinking about Hawk, wondering how I could want anyone more than I wanted this.

My knees nearly buckled when his lips finally pressed to mine. They were soft and warm, dragging a whimper from my throat. His tongue lightly glided over the seam of my lips, and my jaw went slack, my mouth opening. I inhaled sharply when his tongue slid against mine, his palms resting on the sides of my face. Heat moved through my entire body while chills danced down my spine. He kissed me like I was the most precious thing he'd ever touched.

"Fuck, you're sweet," he whispered against my mouth before tilting his head and kissing me deeper.

This time, my legs went weak, and I leaned into him, gripping the front of his shirt as I surrendered to his kiss. I wanted to climb his body. I wanted to make our clothes disappear so I could feel his skin on mine. I wanted to know what other tricks that wicked tongue could do.

I never wanted it to end, but I knew it was going to. Far too soon, in fact, because Hawk pulled back, his forehead resting against mine.

"I want to see you again."

"I don't want to stop seeing you," I whispered.

He chuckled. "We'll figure the rest out."

I was trying to process what that meant—was he referring to Gem and Delaney or something else—when he stepped back, his hands sliding down my arms until he was holding my hands. He stepped back again and released me completely before opening my car door.

I didn't want to leave, but I knew it was for the best. I gave him another smile as I started my car. He closed the door, his eyes on me the entire time. Leaving him filled me with disappointment. I wasn't ready for the date to be over, but as I drove home, I found myself grinning like an idiot. I recalled the entire meal, the conversation, and the way Hawk made me feel. I could honestly say no man had ever made me feel as good as he did.

What I found incredibly interesting was that, for the past hour, not once did I think about Creed.

Then again, thinking about how I didn't think about Creed made me think about him. And now that he had invaded my gray matter, I couldn't get him out of my head.

I suddenly felt guilty. Like I was betraying them both, although when I thought about it rationally, I knew that wasn't the case. It wasn't like I was in a relationship with either of them. Sure, Hawk had dropped the G word earlier, but I knew he was teasing. I wasn't his girlfriend. I mean, I could be. In a heartbeat.

Of course, I could be making more out of it than it was.

But that kiss…

My heart, which had a disturbing tendency to make too much out of nothing, told me I should forget Creed and see where things went with Hawk. But my body was telling me to hold out for a little while longer. I couldn't explain it, not even sure I wanted to.

That night, I dreamed about a mouthwatering UFC fighter who had his wicked way with me while an uber-sexy CEO watched from the shadows. Yeah, maybe some of my wires were getting crossed, but the result was always the same.

16

Creed

As I paced the pristine stone floor of my living room, my hands balled into fists, I told myself that what Hawk did wasn't as bad as I was making it out to be.

I was trying to convince myself that he hadn't violated our most primitive rule, the one stating that if the alpha claimed anyone, as he was entitled to do, his proclamation was final. No one—not a Dominant or a submissive—could challenge him.

Only Hawk *had* violated that rule. He took Journey out tonight, although I'd relayed my intentions. How the fuck could he do that?

He'd be here any minute, and I needed to decide what to do about it. I had two options, one of which involved banning one of my best friends from Primal for life. The other … well, the other was something far more vicious. It involved me beating him until he begged for mercy. Right now, the second option was more appealing because of the red haze clouding my vision.

The sound of the front door opening had me stopping in my tracks. I pivoted to face the foyer, waiting for him to appear. I wanted to see his fucking face … I wanted to know if he even realized what he'd done. I wanted to know if he fucking *cared*.

Hawk appeared, his expression solemn, his back board-straight.

Yeah. He knew what he did.

The only thing he had going for him was his usually smug countenance was missing, his blue eyes holding a river of concern. If there had been one fucking *hint* of a smile, I wouldn't hesitate to toss his ass out of my life once and for all.

It would kill me, by God, but I would do it. Never had Hawk violated a rule like this.

"You better have a damn good explanation," I growled roughly. "Or a fucking apology. You choose."

"I have nothing to apologize for," Hawk said firmly.

His defiance triggered the animal prowling inside me. Before I could stop myself, I rushed him, gripping his throat and slamming him against the wall.

Hawk didn't flinch even as he grunted from the impact.

I held him there, pinned to the wall, my hand tight on his neck, my weight pressed against him. I could hear every deep inhale, every slow exhale.

"Are you telling me you didn't take Journey out tonight?"

His eyes narrowed. "I'm not denying it. I won't apologize for it, either. She was upset. Someone's giving her a hard time at work about talking to us."

"Who?"

"No idea."

I let that sink in, still pinning him in place as I contemplated how to punish him for his transgression. Only the fact that he knew that little detail about Journey made it difficult to focus. He was getting closer to her while I'd managed to keep my distance.

Garrison's words sounded in my head: *I know you're givin' him some rope to hang himself, but you should know it's not a one-sided attraction.*

Goddammit.

"What do you expect me to do about you?" I barked, deflecting my anger outward again.

Hawk's gaze didn't waver. "That's not my call." He leaned his head forward, which put pressure against his neck. "Punish me however you want, Creed. It won't change anything. I'm not giving her up."

There wasn't an ounce of submission in him, which told me so much more than I wanted to know.

"You want this," I accused with a hiss. "You want out."

Hawk shook his head. "I don't, Alpha. That's not what I'm saying."

At least he acknowledged who I was. "What *are* you saying?"

He swallowed, his Adam's apple sliding against my palm. "I've never met a woman like her. She makes me feel … whole again."

That was a jab at me for what went down between us.

My gaze dropped to his mouth, and I found myself staring at his lips. I knew exactly what those lips felt like beneath mine. I knew how fucking good they felt wrapped around my cock. I knew every inch of this man better than I knew anyone else. I'd done things to him that most people would consider cruel and unusual, but those things were what drove both of us. The violent need churned inside us. Although Hawk wanted things I didn't, that didn't change the fact that we were kindred souls. Our desires were reflections of the other.

However, those things Hawk wanted that I didn't … *those* had gotten in the way and resulted in Hawk giving me an ultimatum. I chose to reject it. Since then, Hawk had pushed me on every level. He acted out on purpose, violated rules to get a rise out of me.

And now he had found someone who could put him back together after I had shattered him.

"Are you pushing me on purpose?" I asked, needing to know if this was him getting back at me for how things went down between us.

"No, Alpha. Introducing myself to her was me acting out. Everything after that … I haven't thought about you once." His eyes hardened, and his words were clipped. "When I'm with her, you don't matter, Creed."

That admission caused something in my chest to clench tightly. The pain branched out through my bones, my muscles. It consumed me in a way I didn't expect. I knew Hawk, and I knew he didn't say that to get a rise out of me. He truly believed it.

"You're willing to give me up for her?" I snapped, hating that I was throwing our past back in his face, but I couldn't stop myself. The fury that churned in my veins had me by the balls. I'd say whatever it took to make him feel small.

"I hope it doesn't come to that."

I could hear the sincerity in his tone even though his expression had hardened. What we once shared … the undercurrent still existed. It was a living, breathing thing that caused the air to heat. The hum beneath my skin was still there, even though I had written it off long ago.

"Stay away from her, Hawk," I growled harshly.

His jaw ticked. "I won't do that."

I shoved back, releasing his throat. "You will. This is your only warning."

"You know what, Creed? You can take your warning and shove it up your ass." His face pinched with anger. "You've had plenty of time to make your move, but you haven't. Maybe if you had, I wouldn't have gotten close to her. But I did and…" He shook his head and exhaled slowly. "Whatever this is with her, it feels real to me. Too real to let go of because you want to use the rules of the club in the real world." His jaw bunched again. "You want her? Then I suggest you make your fucking move. We'll let her decide."

I glared.

He glared.

Finally, Hawk said, "Do you intend to punish me? If not, I'm going to bed."

I considered it, but because of my rage, I'd do more harm than good.

"Go," I grumbled.

With that, Hawk spun on his heel and stormed toward the stairs. I stared after him for long minutes. I'd never seen him like this before. Never known Hawk to go to extremes to prove a point. He was a man who was driven by his need to get a reaction. One that he anticipated.

And that told me I had to respond with something he wouldn't see coming.

17

Journey

It was crazy what a solid eight hours of sleep would do.

I woke up this morning with a renewed sense of self thanks to the shuteye and a very insightful conversation I had with my mother last night. After I relayed what I overheard Gem and Delaney saying—which I glossed over and left out the specifics—my mother told me to shove it out of my mind and focus on myself. She reiterated that if I did not have ill intentions, then it didn't matter.

She was right. I don't, and it didn't.

So I decided not to allow Gem or Delaney to confuse my priorities by making assumptions they had no business making. I knew I was not talking to *anyone* for anything more than casual conversation. No promises were being made, no favors being cashed in, only an effort to get to know each other, so I had nothing to feel guilty about. I didn't need special treatment for work because I was more than capable without their help. Plus, what I did on my personal time was no one's business but my own. So if I wanted to have dinner with a handsome man because he asked me to, that was certainly my prerogative.

Granted, that epiphany was overshadowed by an unexpected sense of guilt where Hawk and Creed were concerned. I couldn't figure out what it was I wanted. Despite having very little interaction with Creed, I found myself thinking about him constantly. Even while I'd developed an overwhelming sense of hope where Hawk was concerned. I wanted to pursue whatever this was with him. I wanted to get to know him better, to spend time with him, to take that trip to Vegas one day. Not to get married, of course, but to have that time to ourselves. Whenever I thought about him, my belly twisted with excitement, and I felt like there was something there.

I just needed to stop thinking about Creed and stop anticipating something that was likely never going to happen.

At least, that was what I told myself as I went through my morning routine.

After doing my makeup and adding some curl to my hair, I dressed to impress, although Cheryl had mentioned Fridays were casual. Since I had two product tours on my calendar, I refused to show up in jeans and a T-shirt, opting instead for a khaki mini skirt paired with a form-fitting, long sleeve white shirt. I pull on an oversized faded-green camouflage sweater over it. The "casual" came in because it was designed to hang off one shoulder, and it was short enough to give a peek at the white cotton that covered my belly. I added a pair of light green low-top Chucks, and I was set. It was completely appropriate for work, even if it hadn't been casual Friday, plus it made me feel confident enough to interact with the upper management level I'd need to during the tour.

When I got to work, I was feeling even better since the Friday playlist on my phone included some '80s rock ballads that I knew all the words to. I performed my own version of *Carpool Karaoke* during the drive and got out with a smile on my face.

I maintained that grin past security, greeting Kurt, and as I made my way down to the executive building.

I was only a few feet past the coffee shop when all the fizzing in my veins came to an abrupt halt. The instant I saw Creed strolling toward me with purpose, I was slammed by the same giddy feeling I had whenever I was with Hawk.

If I hadn't already been mesmerized by the dark hair and that granite jaw dusted with at least a day's worth of stubble, I would've done a double-take. The man who wore a suit like it was his own brand of seduction was showcasing his well-built chest and jaw-dropping arms in a black polo—untucked—and a pair of faded distressed jeans that were just loose enough to be stylish but still hugged his tree-trunk legs in the most impressive way. I never would've recognized him from behind, but oh my. I wasn't sure which version of him I liked better, the buttoned-up professional or this casual sex god.

Hoping he was merely late for a meeting, I tried to sidestep, offering a small smile in greeting, but he came to a slow stop directly in front of me.

"Coffee."

It sounded like he was telling me where he was going because it definitely wasn't an offer. I nodded as an acknowledgment that he spoke, then started toward the elevators again, but he stopped me with a gentle hand on my arm.

"That was me inviting you," he said gruffly.

I turned, tilting my head back to make eye contact. "Really?" I couldn't hide my skepticism. "Because it sounded like a statement, not a question."

His eyes crinkled at the corners, but his mouth remained a firm line. He held my gaze for a beat, then nodded toward the coffee shop. When I didn't turn, he urged me that way by tugging my arm.

Not sure what else to do, I started walking with him, expelling the breath I was holding when he released my arm and tucked his hands into his pockets.

"Hawk said you went on a date with him last night."

"I'm not sure it was a date … I mean, it was dinner, but…"

Yeah, I sounded like an idiot. And I felt like one too. More so because I couldn't look him in the eye as I spoke. Why did I deny it? Especially when I'd spent most of last night thinking about Hawk.

"Actually, yes," I said more confidently. "I did go on a date with Hawk last night."

"Did you enjoy yourself?"

"I did."

He stopped walking. "Journey?"

"Hmm?" I asked, looking anywhere but up at him.

"Look at me."

I turned to face him, but my gaze continued to stray to the wall behind him. I couldn't make eye contact, although I didn't know why I felt guilty. It wasn't like he had asked me out or anything.

He chuckled softly, and the next thing I knew, he was gripping my chin with his finger and thumb, gently adjusting my head until my eyes slid to his face. It was such a dominant action, a surprised gasp slipped past my lips as my insides coiled with warmth. I'd never dated a dominant man, but so many of my fantasies revolved around scenarios very much like this one. The mere thought of submitting to Creed Granger had the power to make me lightheaded.

Creed held my stare. "Good girl."

Oh, dear God! The whispered praise spoke to that part of me that had only ever emerged as words on the screen. I inhaled sharply, wishing I could say or do something that would earn me more of his approval.

A second later, I knew I needed to look away because too many people were beginning to trickle into the building. I worried someone would see us, but I was trapped in his stormy gaze, spellbound by what I saw there. He didn't appear at all fazed that I admitted I went on a date with someone he called a friend. Most men would see that as a reason to look elsewhere, but I got the feeling Creed saw it as a challenge.

"What's your preference?"

I was so caught up in his gaze I was confused by the question. "Huh?"

"Coffee preference."

"Oh. Um…" I looked toward the coffee shop, but my eyes were instantly drawn back to his face. "Mocha latte."

"Whipped cream, extra shot?"

"And nonfat milk," I told him, a little taken aback that he knew how I ordered my coffee when I was with Hawk.

"Why nonfat milk *and* whipped cream?"

I grinned. "I like whipped cream, and it's too sweet if you use anything but nonfat milk."

He dug his teeth into his lower lip and studied me as he nodded. "Find a table. I'll get it."

I stared after him for a moment, briefly wondering if I should bolt. Was Creed pulling a dominant card here? Or was that his shining personality coming through? Maybe he didn't know how to be polite, or worse, he didn't know how to phrase a question.

The more disturbing part was how much I liked it.

Since the table Hawk and I had sat at was empty, I headed for that one. It felt familiar, which helped to slow my unruly heart. A little. Okay, not really, but it did give me something to think about that didn't include looking into those all-seeing eyes and getting a glimpse of what I wanted to believe was a hardcore Dominant eager to bend me to his will.

Yeah, yeah. More than likely, I was making something out of nothing, but I couldn't help myself. There was a darkness in Creed that called out to me. I didn't know what it was about him, but I was pulled into his orbit by invisible forces, and even if I could extricate myself, I wasn't sure I would.

My attention drifted over to him, and I noticed he didn't cut the line the way Garrison had. While he stood there, Creed engaged a couple of others in brief conversation as they waited their turn. Each person he spoke with seemed thrilled to have his attention.

I certainly know the feeling.

As I watched him, I couldn't help wondering whether he was privy to the rumors about this place. More specifically, the secret passages beneath the buildings that supposedly led to the most clandestine sex club in the world. Surely he would have to know, right? He couldn't run this place without knowing what went on everywhere, could he? As I'd told Rhylee, he did fit the profile of the dominant who oversaw the club and ruled with a primeval fist, the one they referred to as Alpha.

When Creed approached, he was staring intently, so I shrugged off the absurd thoughts and mentally tucked them away for later.

"Is the coffee free?" I blurted before I could think better of it.

He frowned, but the crease in his forehead disappeared almost immediately. "It is, yes. Why? Did you want one to go?"

"No." I laughed, more than a little flustered. "I was just wondering."

He eased into the chair across from me. "Still haven't read the handbook?"

I was surprised by how much information Hawk had shared with him. At least it answered my earlier question. There was no doubt in my mind they talked often and about everything.

"I got a little preoccupied with the company bio," I answered.

Creed leaned back and propped one ankle on the opposite knee, one wrist resting on the table, his fingers lightly touching his coffee cup. He regarded me like we were old friends. I wished I could be as cool around him, but this man had me tied up in so many knots I might as well have been a macramé bracelet.

"Hawk mentioned someone's giving you a hard time about talking to us."

What were they? A couple of old ladies who sat around and gossiped about me? Jeez.

I waved him off and took a sip of my coffee. "It's nothing. They caught me off-guard yesterday, that's all."

"You've put it behind you?"

"I have."

"So you're not looking at every person who walks by to see if you know them?"

My gaze snapped to his face as I realized I was doing exactly that.

His smirk said he already knew the answer. "If you'd prefer, I'll keep my distance until after the selection is made."

I wasn't sure what confused me more: that Creed Granger was willing to allow rumors and gossip to dictate his actions or that he so readily assumed I would want anything to do with him. I mean, I did, of course. It was even possible I was broadcasting it by the way I was ogling him at every turn, but it was rather presumptuous on his part, right?

"I don't want special treatment," I told him.

He lowered his foot to the floor and leaned forward, resting his forearm on the table. "Special treatment is all you're gonna get, hellcat," he said gruffly, his voice so low that it caused goosebumps on my arms. "But I promise to keep it on a personal basis only."

I think I swallowed my tongue.

Yep. That was what happened. I'd swallowed my tongue, and I was seconds away from choking on it. Was he saying what I thought he was saying?

He sat up straight. "Just know, I make a point never to take a backseat to anything or anyone." He picked up his coffee and stood, those piercing gray eyes still locked on my face as he towered above me. "I damn sure won't do it for long."

With that, Creed walked away, leaving me staring after him with my tongue lodged somewhere in my esophagus.

The day flew by quickly, or it felt like it did. I completed the product tours and even had time to compile my notes before doing a little more research on competitors' products now that I had a better understanding of what we were launching. I didn't chance running into anyone in the cafeteria; instead, eating a protein bar at my desk. I did sneak down for an energy drink at three for a caffeine boost and got lucky that I didn't run into Creed or Hawk. Granted, *lucky* wasn't the word I was thinking at the time because there was no doubt I was disappointed.

Needless to say, I was starting to question my sanity.

"Quick meeting before we head out for the weekend," Cheryl announced as she walked from her office to the team conference area.

I looked up from my computer monitor, realizing it was a summons, not a statement.

I stepped out of my office at the same time Delaney and Gem did, then headed toward the conference table in the center of the space where Cheryl was waiting. Wayne didn't come to work today. According to Cheryl, he had called in sick, claiming he was running a fever. I didn't buy it, but if it was true, I preferred he stayed home, too.

"Your timeline has shifted," she said, looking between the three of us. "Originally, you were going to present to me on Tuesday with time to modify before presenting to the directors. Now you'll be presenting to the VPs and the CEO on Monday afternoon at one o'clock. The directors have been informed. You'll each have thirty minutes. Mr. Weston has also requested you to all be there for each presentation."

"What? Why?" Gem grumbled.

Cheryl stared at them, eyebrows sliding higher. "Which statement are you questioning, Gem?"

"All of it. Why're they moving it up? The launch isn't until the end of the year. It doesn't make sense they're pushing this hard up front."

I had a pretty good idea why, but I didn't offer my input. It wasn't like I could tell them this was my fault. That by pushing Creed off until after the selection was made, he had decided to move up the timeline. He had said he wasn't the sort to take a backseat to anyone or anything. Now I knew how he managed that.

"Does it matter?" Cheryl retorted. "It's their company. Maybe they don't want to put it off any longer."

"But a day? That's—"

"Irrelevant," Cheryl interrupted. "Monday afternoon, you'll be presenting to them. What order do you want to go in?"

"We get to choose?" Delaney asked.

"Yes."

No one spoke up, so I did. "I'll go first."

I think Gem was surprised that I was quick to volunteer. After all, it meant I wouldn't have a chance to get pointers from anyone else.

"Good. Who's next?"

"Wait," Delaney said. "I think Wayne should go first. He's not here to sign up, so why should he get to go last?"

"I agree," Gem noted.

"Fair point. If by chance he brings a doctor's note," Cheryl clarified, "I'll allow him to go last. Otherwise, Wayne's first, Journey's second. Who's third?"

"I'll go third," Delaney offered.

"Perfect. Gem, you'll go last." Cheryl looked between us. "I'll come in an hour early on Monday if you want to go over your presentation. I suggest you find time in your weekend to get it done."

"Well, I guess I know what I'll be doing once my hangover wears off tomorrow," Delaney said as she pivoted and headed back to her office.

I returned to my office and took a seat. Thankfully, the CBD group was the only team I couldn't meet with. Since I had attended the meeting on Wednesday, I felt confident I could do a thorough presentation using only what I'd learned there.

Before I realized what I was doing, I had my phone in my hand, and I was texting Creed.

💬 **WHY DID YOU MOVE THE PRESENTATION?**

His response didn't come for nearly half an hour. At that point, I was walking out of the building with my laptop securely tucked in my bag. I had a lot of work and not a lot of time to do it.

💬 **I TOLD YOU I WOULDN'T WAIT LONG.**

I guess I should've been grateful he didn't have enough notice to move it to today. I would've been completely screwed. Before I could respond, another message came through.

💬 **AND YOU SHOULD KNOW, HAWK'S OFF LIMITS TO YOU THIS WEEKEND, TOO. IF YOU TEXT US, WE WON'T TEXT YOU BACK. GOOD LUCK.**

I stared at my phone screen and frowned. Why did he get to make decisions for Hawk?

💬 **I WASN'T GOING TO TEXT YOU ANYWAY.**

"For some reason, I don't believe you."

I jumped, startled by the gruff voice behind me as I approached my car.

Spinning around, I glared at him. "You know, you could clear your throat or something? Warn a girl."

Creed's smirk was sinful.

"Why'd you move it?" I asked because I was feeling ornery. "The meeting, I mean."

"I shifted my entire calendar by one day."

"Why?"

"So I'd be back in town on Friday."

"What's happening on Friday?"

"You and I are going out."

"That doesn't sound like a request," I informed him, planting my hand on my hip. It wasn't easy to feign irritation when the butterflies in my belly were doing cartwheels.

"Didn't mean for it to."

A black Cadillac Escalade with dark-tinted windows pulled up and stopped behind my car. Creed glanced over at it and nodded before turning his attention back to me.

He reached out and touched my chin. Just the lightest sweep of his knuckle against my skin had my lungs locking down like a maximum security prison.

"Looking forward to Monday, hellcat."

He winked before walking away. I stared after him, mouth agape, as he got into the backseat of the Escalade. The windows were too dark to see in, but I got the feeling he was looking at me as the SUV drove away.

My heart continued to flutter as I watched the Escalade leave the parking lot. But that was nothing compared to the kick it got when I heard an engine revving. I turned to see Hawk a few feet away, straddling his motorcycle, his helmet propped in front of him. He sat up straight, smiled, then crooked his finger in that gesture to beckon someone.

Without so much as a thought, I walked toward him.

"Creed told me you're off limits to me this weekend."

His grin widened. "He's not wrong. But I wasn't gonna risk not getting a kiss to tide me over for the next two days."

Oh, boy. I think my heart might've fluttered right out of my chest.

Hawk curled his hand around my neck and pulled me toward him as he leaned over. His mouth met mine, and instantly my mind was blank. I existed only on a plane of sensation as pleasure coursed through my veins. His kiss had just the right amount of dominance to make me believe he was in control. And the way his thumb caressed my cheek filled me with warmth.

"It's gonna be a long fucking weekend," he whispered against my mouth.

"Maybe."

Hawk pressed a gentle kiss to my lips before releasing me. He took a deep breath, his eyes imploring me like he was trying to memorize my face. That single moment felt like both a lifetime and a millisecond. Neither felt long enough.

"I guess I'll see you on Monday."

"You definitely will."

I stepped back as he pulled his helmet on. The visor was closed, but I could feel his eyes on me. I was hesitant to look away. I didn't want to let go of this moment.

With a single head nod, he took off. I spun to watch him the same way I had watched Creed's SUV, following until Hawk left the parking lot.

"Oh, girl," I muttered softly. "You are in so much trouble."

Two hours later, I was sitting at my parents' dining room table, my laptop open, my iPad set up beside it, and my phone just out of reach. I was doing research on my iPad while building my presentation on the laptop. As for my phone … I was doing everything in my power not to reach for it to see if, by chance, Creed or Hawk had texted me.

I knew they hadn't because there were no messages the last time I checked. Three minutes ago.

Exhaling harshly, I flopped back in the chair and glared at the presentation on the screen. My gaze swung to my phone, and before I could think about it, I grabbed it. Only this time, I didn't check my text messages. Instead, I pulled up Rhylee's number and hit the call button.

"What's up, chickadee?" Rhylee chirped.

"You're in a good mood," I said, realizing it sounded more like an accusation than an assessment.

She laughed. "I am. I met my word goal every day this week. I'm having wine to celebrate."

"We should have wine at Austere," I suggested, my insides clenching. Part of me was hoping she would decline because Rhylee *always* declined an invitation to go out. But at the same time, I was hoping she wouldn't. I needed to get out of the house, or I'd go insane.

"Austere? Seriously?"

"Yes," I decided firmly.

She sounded suspicious when she said, "Why?"

I shrugged, although she couldn't see me. "It's been a long week, and I know you've been wanting to go. I need something to take my mind off … work." And Hawk. And Creed.

She didn't respond, but I could practically hear Rhylee's brain spinning. She'd been suggesting we go to Austere for the better part of the last six months, ever since I told her there was a chance it was connected to the secret club. I had never actually found any proof that the two were linked by anything other than proximity, but there'd been rumors. I figured if there were a way to sway her to my side, the cigar lounge would be it. And I was all for using every tool in my arsenal.

"Okay," Rhylee finally said.

"Okay? Really?"

There was a smile in her voice now. "Yes. Let's do it. We'll go, have a nice dinner, some wine, and check out the scenery."

I exhaled with relief. "I'll take an Uber to your apartment. We'll go from there."

"I can be the designated driver. I've only had a few sips," Rhylee offered.

"No. If we're doing this, we're doing it right."

Rhylee chuckled. "Damn right we are."

After telling her I'd see her in an hour, I disconnected the call and raced upstairs to see if I'd brought anything worthy of a night out at a cigar bar.

Then I realized I didn't even know what one would wear to a cigar bar.

18

Creed

It was still early for a Friday night, but I was beginning to feel the hum of the weekend warriors who liked to kick things off with a bang. The slow trickle of customers had turned into a steady stream, and with each passing minute, more and more people appeared. By midnight, we'd be close to capacity, which was all I could hope for.

The customers were filling the lower level, scattered throughout at dining tables and in the public lounge areas. The members-only section was nearly at capacity, although we hadn't started allowing people into the VIP section on the second floor, where I'd been for the past half hour.

"…with her at the helm, I think the rollout will be a success."

Garrison's voice faded when I saw *her* walk through the doors.

At first, I noticed only the long, silky blond hair and the short black dress, but instantly, I knew it was Journey. She was with another woman, who I recognized as Rhylee Graham from pictures I had found when Ryder first told me about his daughter's mission to discover the truth about Primal. At the time, I'd wanted to know who I was up against, and getting information on the friends Journey had roped in to help her had been easy enough. If I recalled correctly, this one was a published author. She wrote romance novels about BDSM, and as soon as I had unearthed that, my quest for information died a lonely death. It explained her curiosity and her need for details, so I cataloged her as harmless.

I wasn't sure Journey qualified as harmless, considering the obsession I'd formed, but I didn't believe she was a threat to the club or its members. I was curious whether she had a penchant for BDSM like her friend did, though. I hadn't considered it until now. Perhaps there was a chance she was closer to my world than I initially thought.

One thing was for sure, their presence here told me they were still digging, likely following up on the rumor I started many months ago. They were mistaken if they thought they'd find anything at Austere that tied back to Primal. The closest they'd get was to sit in the same section with or possibly be served by a club member. Not that they would know since the members of Primal were sworn to secrecy. Their loyalty was guaranteed by an iron-clad nondisclosure agreement designed to reduce them to nothing if they discussed anything related to Primal.

Regardless of why Journey was here, I couldn't deny it satisfied me in a way I didn't expect. I'd resigned myself to getting through the weekend without seeing her or hearing her voice. It would be her last reprieve because come next week, I had every intention of pursuing Journey Zeplyn the way I should've been since the beginning.

"Isn't that…?" Garrison prompted.

"Yeah." I didn't take my eyes off Journey as they talked animatedly with the hostess. The best guess was they didn't have reservations.

I pulled out my cell phone and dialed the floor manager.

"Yes, boss?"

"Two ladies at the front door. Blonde and brunette. Seat them."

"Of course, boss," he answered quickly.

I disconnected and continued to watch until they were seated personally by the floor manager at a two-seater booth along the short wall. I didn't know if it was luck or happenstance, but Journey was facing away from me, which allowed me to stare without worrying she'd see me.

For the next half hour, I managed small talk with Garrison while I watched Journey, noting what she was eating and drinking. It was borderline stalkerish, but I didn't give a fuck. I wanted to know every detail about this woman. How she took her coffee, which wine she preferred, her favorite dish, whether she liked flowers or jewelry or both. Those were just the beginning.

I continued to watch as she talked animatedly with her friend. She was so open and carefree; it was refreshing to see. I didn't think she even realized the attention she was getting from several men sitting in the vicinity. Every time she laughed, someone looked her way, and I'd seen more than one hungry stare lingering a little too long for my taste.

I took a sip of whiskey, then glanced over my shoulder when I heard footsteps.

Hawk approached, looking wary. His attitude from last night had dissipated. I was grateful because I didn't want to talk about what had happened. It was the first time Hawk had stood up to me. When it mattered, anyway. And in a sense, he was right. I hadn't made my move, and that was on me. If I had, perhaps I'd have a leg to stand on when I accused him of overstepping. It didn't help my case that Journey wasn't a member of my club; therefore, the rules didn't apply.

That didn't mean I was going to make it easy on Hawk.

"Who's Journey with?" Garrison asked.

"Rhylee Graham," I answered, still watching Journey.

"You know her?"

"Never met her." I glanced his way. "She's helping Journey dig into the club."

Garrison smirked, his attention shifting back to her. "That right?"

I gave him a few highlights from my research—she was a romance author, thirty-two years old, originally from Texas, had lived in California for nine years.

"Has Nick seen her yet?"

I looked over. "No idea. Why?"

Garrison popped his eyebrows. "She's just his type."

I looked back at Rhylee, trying to see what he was referring to, and that was when I noticed it.

Rhylee Graham was a sexier version of Nick's ex-wife and at least a handful of his ex-girlfriends. He had a penchant for redheads with slamming bodies, but unlike the others, Rhylee had an edge I suspected she kept under wraps as much as possible. I wasn't sure how successful she was at hiding it, considering I could see a wealth of tattoos covering every inch of skin exposed by that tight dress.

Yeah, I could see Nick being completely infatuated with her. And the fact that she wrote BDSM novels... How could he possibly go wrong?

"He coming tonight?" I asked Garrison.

"Should be here shortly. Why?"

"No reason." This should be interesting.

I glanced back to see Hawk standing behind me. His full attention was on Journey, and based on his rigid stance, he was gearing up to make a really bad decision.

To keep that from happening, I snapped my fingers and pointed to the floor. "Kneel."

His eyes darted to my face, his eyebrows lowering. His desire to defy me glittered hotly in his blue eyes, but I also saw another emotion churning. This one was far more powerful than the need to fight.

"Don't make me tell you again, or I'll collar you and chain you to the fucking wall," I said firmly.

He moved over to my side and kneeled on the carpeted floor beside my chair. He didn't look at me, nor did he bow his head the way he would've if he weren't looking to be punished.

"Do not let me catch you anywhere near her tonight," I said, keeping my voice low and even. "If I do, your ass will become reacquainted with the cane. And I promise you won't sit the entire weekend. I'll make sure of it. Do you understand me?"

He grunted.

His lack of respect was irritating, but I was giving him a reprieve. It was difficult not to, considering I completely understood his fascination with Journey. I was equally as fascinated.

When the waitress returned with refills, I motioned her closer.

"See those two women down there? The blonde and brunette?"

She nodded, following my gaze.

"Their meals and drinks are on the house tonight. Take care of it."

"Yes, Alpha," she said softly before quietly leaving us.

Not all of the waiters and waitresses at Austere were Primal members, but several were. Those were the ones who took care of me when I was here because they didn't ask questions, and I didn't have to worry about someone hearing or seeing something they might find offensive. Such as a grown man kneeling on the carpet.

Laughter from the main floor drew my attention. I noticed Journey's head was tipped back, and that sexy sound was coming from her.

Yeah, it was safe to say I'd formed an addiction to her laugh. My fate had been sealed the first time I heard it.

"Is it your plan to pretend you're not here?" Garrison goaded.

"We're off limits to her this weekend," I explained.

He chuckled. "Her choice or yours?"

"Both."

Hawk grunted beside me.

"Quiet. Another sound out of you, and I'll shove something in that mouth to ensure you're quiet."

His head snapped to the side, his gaze slamming into me. It was a damn good thing I was only looking at him from the corner of my eye. Otherwise, he might've seen right through me. I hadn't intended to say that, and I damn sure didn't mean it the way it sounded. I hadn't laid a finger on him for seven fucking months, and I didn't intend to. I figured any second now, I'd get past my infatuation with Hawk and the pleasure it brought me to dominate him. Truth was, I'd never cared much for dominating men, submissive or not. I had because my role as Alpha required I dominated all members of the club when it was warranted. However, no one had ever sparked my need to control the way Hawk did.

But Hawk had made his decision. He shunned me when I wouldn't agree to more than what I had to offer in my role as Alpha. I didn't pretend I was looking for anything more than pleasure and pain, the fuel for my primal instincts. I wasn't capable of giving anything more than that. Certainly not anything deeper. Having been an orphan, I'd grown accustomed to not having anyone to call my own. I considered myself lucky to have the friends I had. But more than that … it wasn't in the cards for me.

When my cock twitched at the thought of sliding deep into Hawk's throat, I got to my feet.

"He's not to move," I told Garrison. "I want someone watching him at all times."

"Got it," Garrison nodded. "Tell the ladies I said hello."

I ignored him, then made my way down the staircase that led to the main floor. I knew I shouldn't, but I couldn't resist walking over to greet Journey. I'd already determined she made me do things I would never have before, and I was tired of fighting it. The past five days had been a hell I didn't wish to repeat, and if I kept it up, I'd lose my damn mind before I ever got my hands on her.

I wandered the main floor, greeting the guests I recognized and checking in with a few I didn't before I made my way to Journey's table. Her friend noticed me first, and when her eyes landed on my face, I saw the recognition, not to mention the ingrained instinct to submit. Unlike Hawk, it appeared Rhylee had done her homework on how to greet a Dominant. Her eyes lowered briefly, her head tilting downward, averting her gaze. She wasn't a natural, but it was clear she believed she was worthy.

What she didn't realize was I preferred my submissives to have a backbone. I didn't want a woman who stood obediently at my side or knelt at my feet in public. I wasn't looking for one who wanted to dedicate their life to ensuring they didn't incite me, nor did I want a doll to play with. In my world, it was all about the chase.

"Good evening," I greeted when I stepped up to the table, earning Journey's attention.

Journey gasped softly, clearly surprised to see me. "Creed."

"Journey." I smiled at her, then looked at her friend. "And you must be Rhylee."

Her eyes shifted to Journey, then back to me. "Yes … I … uh … yes, Sir."

I offered my hand so I could formally introduce myself. "I'm Creed Granger, the proprietor of this establishment. It's a pleasure to meet you."

"You, too, Sir," she whispered, her gaze locked on my hand. I tried to release hers, but she held on for a few additional seconds. Looked as though she hadn't read *every* page of the *Good Submissive Handbook*. Not that there was one. Or hell, maybe there was.

"I don't care for honorifics," I informed her, keeping my voice low. "Call me Creed."

She nodded, looking appropriately chastised, which wasn't my intention.

I turned back to Journey, who was staring at me as though I'd grown another eyeball, this one on my forehead. If I wasn't mistaken, there was a glint of fury in her brilliant blue eyes.

"Is there anything I can get you?"

She swallowed, her eyes finally shifting away from me. "No. We're doing fine. Thank you."

I didn't bother hiding my amusement. "Very well. I'll talk to you later."

I walked away, enjoying the fact that my mere presence made her nervous.

19

Journey

"Oh, my God," Rhylee whispered, leaning across the table as Creed walked away. "Do you realize who that is?"

"I met him, remember?" I retorted a little too harshly.

"I know." She stared after him, her chin resting on her hand.

She looked at him like he deserved to be on a pedestal so all the world could worship at his feet. Right now, I wanted to knock him upside the head with a book. Who did he think he was holding my friend's hand a little longer than necessary for a polite introduction? Was he rubbing it in that he was always just out of reach? Maybe that was his point.

If I had to wager a guess, I'd say he was drawn to Rhylee's submissive side. The fact that she called him Sir likely put his head in the clouds. It didn't explain why he called her on it, but maybe that was how it worked between a Dom and a submissive. Maybe he made up the rules as they went along. By the end of the night, I was sure he'd be ordering her to her knees, having her—

"I can't believe you told him about me." She was still looking after him.

I didn't correct her, but it did make me wonder how he knew who she was. Had he looked into me?

"I swear we shared a moment," Rhylee declared. "The look in his eyes when I called him Sir. And then the way he corrected me. So passionate."

Passionate? I was thinking more along the lines of rude, but hey, *potato, potahto.*

Rhylee sighed dreamily, staring after Creed as he stopped at another table to chat with a few men talking over drinks.

"He's the one they call Alpha," she mused. "I can feel it in my bones. My inner submissive felt his power, his need to dominate." She looked over at me. "We should move to the lounge when we're finished."

Not five minutes ago, Rhylee had suggested we go back to her apartment and drink wine there. "I thought you were ready to go."

Rhylee shook her head. "I don't want to miss my chance to talk to him again."

Oh, boy.

His dark, decadent voice still sounded in my head as though he'd planted it there to taunt me. I couldn't resist looking over at him one more time. He caught me staring when he glanced back before he moved on to greet more customers.

Was Rhylee right? Was he the Alpha of Primal? Could it be that easy? Had I unveiled the truth without even trying? Were the rumors about the secret passageways that led from this place to the Primal Instincts offices true, too? Or was it all bullshit meant to drum up business or make Creed Granger look mysterious?

More importantly, why did I even care? I saw the way he had held Rhylee's hand. Clearly, he'd found something that intrigued him, and it wasn't me. I wouldn't pretend I knew the first thing about being a submissive. I found the premise fascinating, sure, but that was all it was to me. A fascination that I could enjoy from hearsay and fiction. I'd never bowed my head or called anyone Sir or Master. I wasn't even sure I could. Not without laughing. So maybe I should give up this nonsense altogether. What would finding the club do for me anyway?

"Can we get the check?" Rhylee said.

It was then I realized our waiter had returned. I tore my gaze away from Creed to look up at the man.

"Your meals and drinks are on the house tonight, courtesy of Mr. Granger."

"Oh." Rhylee giggled. "That's very kind of Creed."

I found myself grinding my teeth together at her use of his first name. I shoved it aside, remembering I was looking into the club to sate my curiosity; she was the submissive seeking a Dom. Who was I to come between her and the man she'd been fantasizing about? Granted, I wasn't sure she'd actually fantasized about Creed, but rather a fictional Dominant she'd created in her mind. Probably made sense that she would immediately snag Creed as her muse for that character.

"We'd like to move to the lounge if that's all right," Rhylee told the waiter.

"Of course. Let me see what's available. I'll be right back."

"Can you believe Creed is comping our dinner?" Rhylee asked in that loud whisper again. If she thought she was being subtle, she was wrong. "What did you tell him about me, anyway?"

I stared at her, unable to come up with a lie that would benefit her or me. Try as I might, I couldn't shake my misplaced anger. She didn't deserve that. I needed a moment to collect my thoughts. Privately.

"I … uh … I need to use the restroom. I'll find you in the lounge when I come back."

She nodded excitedly. "Wish me luck. I'm going to try to talk to Creed again."

I injected as much cheer in my tone as I could muster. "Good luck."

I managed a smooth pace as I walked across the main floor toward the back corner where the bathrooms were located. I didn't notice anything or anyone as I walked, my focus on the *stupid, stupid, stupid* mantra currently on replay in my head. I should've known Creed was messing with me. He probably took my spending time with Hawk as a challenge like I initially thought. I wouldn't be surprised if he flirted with every woman he met. He probably had a different one in his bed every single night.

I was such an idiot.

I reached the bathroom and slipped inside. Unfortunately, it wasn't empty because an attendant was standing near the sinks, likely prepared to offer me a paper towel to dry my hands when I was finished. I smiled at her as I skimmed the large space, the half-dozen stalls, the gold accents, the mosaic-tiled walls, the marble floors. It was as luxurious as the rest of the place. There were even vanities lit with large LED-lined mirrors and boxes of tissues discreetly hidden beneath marble covers.

I nodded at the attendant and moved toward the vanities. I stopped to look at myself, disliking the woman I saw staring back at me. I was a failure as a friend, and that bothered me. I couldn't believe I harbored animosity toward Rhylee simply because she found Creed attractive. I mean, he *was* attractive. She had every right to want to get to know him better.

Taking a deep breath, I tried to calm my rattled nerves. I simply needed to pretend I didn't care. Eventually, it would become second nature, and I'd move on with my life. When Rhylee invited me to her wedding to Creed, I'd be able to gladly accept the offer to be a bridesmaid. Maybe Hawk would even be my date.

Oh, who was I kidding? I just wanted to go home, crawl into bed, and wallow in my self-pity. After *that*, maybe I'd be able to accept that—

The door to the bathroom opened, and I reached into my clutch to retrieve my lipstick, hoping to look like I was freshening up and not scolding myself over my actions. When I looked up, I inhaled sharply as I slowly turned around to face Creed.

"Excuse us," he told the attendant, not looking at her.

"Yes, sir," she said politely before making a hasty exit.

When we were alone, I looked past him at the door. "What are you doing in here? Shouldn't you be out there getting to know my friend better? I mean, she was hoping to get a chance to talk to you. *Sir.*"

He moved closer.

Slowly, seductively, he closed the gap between us until I was forced to tilt my head back to peer up at him. Not only was he ridiculously tall, he was *big*. His chest was broad, his arms thick. I was pretty sure those enormous biceps were the size of my thighs.

I didn't usually fantasize about big men. Probably because I'd always wondered about the logistics. I came up to his shoulder, but only because I was wearing heels. Barefoot, I'd likely reach his armpit. He outweighed me by at least a hundred pounds. I couldn't even imagine holding his hand because his fingers were so long, so wide... My thoughts instantly shifted to his cock. Was he as well-endowed? Would he split me in two if we ever...?

I shook off the absurd thought, hating that my cheeks were warming as though Creed could hear my inner musings.

Creed didn't seem too worried about potentially intimidating me because he stepped forward until I could feel the denim covering his legs brushing my knees.

"I don't want Rhylee, hellcat."

That wasn't the first time he had called me that, and I had to wonder why. Thankfully, I didn't ask. I wasn't sure I could survive his reasoning.

"Could've fooled me. You seemed to enjoy holding her hand."

A sinful smirk slowly formed on his beautiful mouth, his eyes creasing at the corners. He really was an attractive man.

"Are you jealous?"

"Of course not," I lied.

His eyes shimmered with amusement. "I like that you are."

This time when he stepped forward, I took one step back. I bumped the edge of the vanity behind me, finding myself trapped. I doubted my body should be heating, my pussy clenching from the vivid imagery that ran through my mind as I imagined myself beneath him, our sweat-slick bodies moving as one.

What was *wrong* with me?

When he leaned down, my breath hitched, and my nipples hardened. My pussy spasmed, a reminder that I couldn't even remember what it felt like to have a cock inside me, and right then, I would've done just about anything to have this man remind me.

He tilted his head, his lips hovering dangerously close to mine. I could smell his cologne—musk, sandalwood, and mandarin. It was intoxicating.

"Creed…"

"Don't worry. I'm holding to my promise."

I could feel his breath on my lips, and I swayed, my brain fuzzy as I tried to process his words.

I frowned. "What promise?"

"Off limits, remember?"

I pulled my head back so I could meet his gaze. "Seriously?"

That devilish smirk returned as he took a step back. "I just wanted to see for myself if it's mutual."

"If *what's* mutual?"

"This attraction."

My insides coiled, the tension more potent than anything I'd ever felt. Hearing Creed admit he was attracted to me sent a surge of electricity through my veins.

His hands remained in his pockets, and I wondered if he was as casual as he appeared or if that was his way of keeping his hands to himself. Then again, he didn't have to touch me for me to feel the physical caress. It came from the sweep of his gaze as he looked at me.

"It's not mutual." Oh, the lies just kept on coming.

His eyes glittered with promise, but he didn't say anything.

"Like you, I don't get hung up on anyone for too long." Feigning a casualness I didn't feel, I turned around to face the mirror, avoiding his gaze in the reflective glass as I reached for my lipstick. "I came here tonight to find someone else to spend my time with."

The words were barely out of my mouth when he pressed up against me, his arm circling me, his hand curling across my throat, pulling me into him. He didn't do it slowly; if he had, I wasn't sure it would've had the same impact. The move surprised me, but more than that, it sent lust on a collision course through my entire body. So much so that I had to question my reaction because an insanely disturbing arousal followed it.

Creed's big hand spanned my neck as his thumb pressed under my chin, forcing my head back. I drew in a ragged breath when it registered that his hard body was pressed intimately against my back. And his muscles weren't the only parts of him that was hard.

"Look at me," he growled softly.

My head wasn't back enough to look up and see him, so I had to divert my gaze to the mirror.

"What about Hawk?" he asked when our eyes met in the reflective glass.

"What about him?"

"You willing to give him up?"

I frowned. "No."

His surprise registered for only a single heartbeat. Then it was gone.

"You should know I'm a very possessive man, hellcat." He squeezed, not enough to cut off my air, but enough to hold my attention. "Very possessive."

I wasn't sure whether he meant that as a threat, but I heard a promise. Or maybe I was losing my mind because, again, I shouldn't have been turned on by his high-handedness. I shouldn't like the aggressiveness of his stance or the way he held me there.

Only I was, and I did.

"You can't have both."

"Sure I can," I countered. It was one thing to be turned on by his physical dominance, but I damn sure was not turned on by his desire to tell me what I could and couldn't do.

"Is that what you want? Both?"

"Maybe."

I was still holding his stare when his grip on my neck loosened, his fingers sweeping across my skin. I watched as he slid my hair off my shoulder, dragging it aside. I swore I was on the verge of orgasm when he leaned down and kissed my neck. The warmth of his lips made my pussy clench and my skin tingle. And when his teeth scraped across my over-sensitized flesh, I shuddered, somehow managing to bite back my request for him to keep doing that.

His words whispered over my neck. "For his sake, I suggest you avoid getting intimate with Hawk. I can't guarantee his safety if you do."

I whimpered, the sound dying in my throat when he stood tall. He held my gaze in the mirror, a sexy smirk forming on his mouth.

"Looking forward to seeing you on Monday, hellcat."

"You're an asshole," I hissed, hating that he was walking away while I was practically going up in flames.

A squeak escaped me when he grabbed my arm and spun me around. A second later, he had me perched on the vanity, standing between my legs, one big hand curled under my thigh, the other firmly gripping my jaw. My breath left my body in a rush, my temperature skyrocketed, and a lake was developing between my legs.

A normal response would've been fear, but I wasn't scared of him. No, this was most definitely not fear that was flooding my bloodstream. It was adrenaline fueled by lust. Never had I had this sort of reaction to anyone. It was the aggression, the way he manhandled me. It triggered something inside me, flipped a switch, started an engine.

"You want me to take care of that ache between your legs," he growled roughly, his big hand sliding higher, his thumb brushing the inside of my thigh. "I will, hellcat. Just say the word."

The word. The word. The word.

Thankfully, my inner hussy was on mute. Otherwise, I would've been in trouble right about now.

"I'd never make it that easy for you," I countered.

His eyes darkened as he dragged in a ragged breath. "I'm hoping you won't."

A warning bell sounded in my head. My fight-or-flight instinct kicked in, balancing precariously like a seesaw holding the same weight on both ends. A feather would tip it one way or another, but I wasn't sure which side I wanted it to fall on. The urge to fight him was powerful, but the need to run was equally so. He would win in a fight and catch me if I fled, so either choice was moot. But it was the thrill that intoxicated me.

Creed growled, a dark rumble deep in his throat that made my clit swell and throb.

"Are you scared, kitten?"

I nodded because I would've been a fool not to tell him the truth. But I didn't tell him I wasn't scared of him, but rather of this insane feeling I had when I was near him.

His smile was sin and sex. "You should be because I'm the man who'll take everything you're willing to give and convince you to give me more. And when you don't, I'll make you. You violate the rules, I'll punish you. You run, I'll chase you. You hold back, I'll break you."

I was pretty sure I just spontaneously combusted.

I think he was trying to warn me off, but all he managed to do was make me burn hotter, brighter. He hadn't touched me anywhere else, but I felt like his hands had roamed every inch of my body. I felt like he was inside me and on me at the same time. I was consumed by him, mesmerized by the heat that burned in his gaze, the seduction in his words, and the strength in his body.

I drew air deep into my lungs as I held his stare. "Break me, Creed. I dare you."

His grip on my jaw tightened as he leaned down. He hovered so close I could feel the warmth of his breath, smell the richness of his cologne. He tilted my head so our lips were angled for maximum penetration, but still, he didn't kiss me. My entire body was awash in sensation. I could feel him under my scalp and beneath my toenails. He was everywhere at once, even while he was nowhere.

"I don't break my promises, kitten," he whispered against my lips. "You asked for space. I'm giving it to you."

Suddenly, his warmth disappeared as he released me. I remained on the vanity as he stood tall.

"I'll see you on Monday," he said.

This time I didn't call him names as he left, and I was still staring at the door a minute later when the attendant returned.

Somehow I managed to pull myself together enough to face my friend. Or at least that was my intention when I returned, searching for Rhylee in the lounge. I found her sitting in a chair, a glass of wine in her hand and a blinding smile on her face as she talked softly to Nick Weston.

I slowly walked toward them, waiting for either to notice me. I was nearly in front of them when Nick looked up, causing Rhylee to do the same.

"Hey. You're back." She smiled brightly. "Journey Zeplyn, this is Nick Weston. He works at Primal Instincts."

"We've—"

"It's a pleasure to meet you," Nick said, cutting me off as he got to his feet and held out a hand.

"I was in the new hire class," I informed him, shaking his hand as though this was our first introduction.

"I thought you looked familiar."

I noticed Rhylee staring at him as though he had descended from the heavens, and she was gearing up to worship at his feet. It was a look very similar to the one she'd given Creed earlier, only this time, I didn't feel defensive, I felt relieved.

"I … uh…" I cleared my throat. "I think I'm going to head home. I've got a work project due on Monday, and I need to work on it for a while."

"Oh. Okay, yeah," Rhylee said, her tone filled with disappointment.

Rhylee started to get up, but I held up a hand. If it were any other place, I would've never even considered leaving my friend behind. However, I knew Nick wouldn't let anything happen to her. She was safe here.

"I'll call an Uber. You stay; enjoy yourself." I smiled at Nick. "She's my best friend. Take good care of her."

Nick winked, and Rhylee blushed.

They were cute.

"Call me tomorrow," I told Rhylee before heading for the door.

I was almost home free when I felt Creed's eyes on me. How I knew it was him, I wasn't sure, but I was certain he was tracking me across the room. Before I could reach fresh air, he strolled up to my side, opening the door so I could exit.

"Thank you," I said as I pulled my phone from my purse. "I'll just wait outside until my Uber arrives."

"Put that away," he said, motioning to my phone.

Before I could ask why, the sleek blacked-out Escalade that Creed had been in earlier pulled up to the curb. Creed put a hand on my lower back and guided me forward. He opened the rear passenger door, then stepped back so I could get in.

"Tell Mason where you need to go. He'll ensure you get there safely."

I was staring at Creed's mouth as he spoke, wishing I had the nerve to kiss him because I knew he wasn't going to kiss me.

Creed leaned in, his mouth close to my ear. "Good night, hellcat. Sweet dreams."

For the record, there was nothing sweet about my dreams that night. Nothing sweet at all.

20

Hawk

KNEELING ON THE FLOOR FOR TWO HOURS was hell. I knew because it felt like my patellas had been crushed into dust. Thankfully, two hours was as long as I'd had to endure before I found an opening to make my escape.

And if you're rolling your eyes thinking it was insane for a grown man—an MMA champion with a 2nd-dan black belt in Kyokushin Karate and a 2nd-degree black belt in Brazilian Jiu-Jitsu, at that—to kneel on the floor because a man told him to … well, keep right on rolling them because I won't apologize for my actions. I accepted this was my place in the world a long damn time ago, and I wouldn't fucking trade it for anything. Even if it was fucking complicated.

Garrison had left early, passing his babysitting duties to Nick. That lasted until Nick caught sight of Journey's friend, the sexy redhead with the big tits. I might've mentioned she was single, although I honestly had no fucking idea. I simply needed an escape route, and his interest in her provided the opening. At that point, it was merely a matter of waiting until Creed was preoccupied with God knows who in the members-only room.

Not that I cared. I didn't have it in me to give a shit what Nick, Garrison, or Creed were doing or who they were with. Well, maybe Creed, but only because I knew if I didn't pay the piper tonight, my punishment for going out to dinner with Journey would be significantly more painful tomorrow. As it was, I was surprised he hadn't done something last night. And while there were times I craved the game, I wasn't sure anyone could handle what Creed had in store for me. I'd never seen him react as he did last night when he learned I'd taken Journey out for burgers. That simple date had set the man off in a way no other woman had ever triggered him.

So, I guess it made sense that he hadn't punished me. Perhaps Creed's moral compass wasn't calibrated like most people, but he still had one. And there were lines he wouldn't cross.

As for his reaction… I got it. I did. I knew exactly what he felt because I'd never felt this way about a woman before, either. Regardless of his feelings, I intended to continue my quest to get to know Journey. But treading lightly where Creed was concerned was a requirement if I wanted to continue breathing.

Hence the reason I followed his instruction and didn't talk to Journey while she was at Austere. I was damn tempted. Thankfully, the temptation was eradicated when she left a short while ago.

With nothing keeping me there, I decided to call it a night, slipping out without saying a word to anyone. I took the scenic route home. The guard at the gate recognized me, waving me through. When I arrived at the house, the private security gate opened automatically, granting me access. Like most nights, I parked outside. The garage was plenty big, easily holding every vehicle the three of us owned. But calling it a garage was equivalent to calling the Hope diamond a rock.

It was midnight by the time I finished taking a shower and pulling on a pair of sweatpants. I didn't bother with a shirt, figuring I'd have to strip for Creed's punishment anyway. This way, there was less work that went into it for me.

I went back downstairs and camped out on the couch while I waited, flipping channels on the television mounted into the nook beside the enormous fireplace. The house was eerily silent and dark, the lights of the city below not bright enough to penetrate the glass walls.

I was still channel-surfing two hours later when the door from the garage opened. I propped myself up, peering over the back of the sofa, waiting for Creed to appear. He would've seen the motorcycle in the driveway, so he knew I was there. Proven when he stepped into view, his gaze sweeping the lower level before landing on me.

I didn't say a word. I knew better. There was enough tension in his shoulders as it was. I had no desire to push him further. A smart move on my part since, when he moved closer, I noticed there was something different about him. He looked more intense than usual.

As he approached, he reached behind his head and gripped the collar of his shirt before pulling it off in one smooth move. Admiring him was something I tried not to do as much as I could. After all, it was a futile endeavor, considering Creed wanted nothing to do with me anymore. At one point, I would've been waiting for him for more pleasurable reasons. Now, I settled for his punishment to remind myself that I was the one who had fucked this up. If I hadn't wanted more from him, there was a good chance he would still be using me for his own pleasure.

I swallowed as he revealed the impressive body I hadn't seen nearly enough of lately. I didn't have to catalog the tattoos that covered his chest and back because I knew each and every one by heart.

"Sit up," he commanded, his voice thundering through the cavernous space.

I clicked the power button on the remote to turn off the television, then dropped my feet to the floor as he stepped around the sofa.

"You don't get to run tonight," he said, his tone gravel-rough. "Tonight, you obey."

My natural instinct was to argue and to fight, but I refrained even as my muscles tensed to flee. I kept my eyes forward, resisting the urge to look at his face. When he stopped directly in front of me, I got an unobstructed view of him releasing the clasp on his belt. The sound the leather made as it slid out of the loops was overly loud in the room. He flipped the button free, then lowered his zipper. I swore I could hear the teeth as they disengaged slowly.

Behind the fly of his jeans, Creed's cock was impressively large, stretching the fabric of his black Tom Ford boxer briefs.

In my position, I was at eye level with his crotch, which was clearly what he wanted. I was forced to watch as he pushed his jeans down, his feet spreading wide to keep them from slipping down his thighs. His hand slid into his underwear, fingers curling securely around his shaft as he used his free hand to push them down. His dick was proportionate to his oversized body. Long and thick, I knew from experience it required patience to take him the way he preferred, whether in my mouth or my ass.

As for his intentions, I couldn't have guessed. I hadn't had intimate contact with this man in seven months, nor had I anticipated it. The fact that he was willing told me he was at the end of his rope, something that wasn't normal for him. Creed Granger was the most controlled man I'd ever met. Nothing rattled him.

With the exception of one tiny woman.

"We'll call this punishment by proxy," Creed said, his voice deep.

I took that to mean he was punishing Journey. For what, though? And why was he taking it out on me? I kept the questions to myself. It wasn't like I would tell him no. I'd never refused this man, and I never would.

Creed palmed the back of my head and jerked me forward. I followed the momentum, sliding off the sofa, my knees hitting the hard floor with a thud, my feet shifting to the left. I was trapped between his legs and the sofa, the position awkward and uncomfortable, which was clearly his intention. It didn't matter. The pain would eventually go away, but the moment wouldn't.

I planted my hands on my thighs, palms up to signify my complete obedience. Creed's hand slid to the top of my head, his thumb pressing on my forehead as he forced me to look up, my neck stretching uncomfortably. I stared at his face as he angled his cock down, pushing past my lips. I let him in, opening wide. I didn't lick or suck; I merely gave him an orifice to use for his pleasure.

He grunted, his grip tightening on my head the deeper he slid into my mouth. When his cockhead bumped the back of my throat, I focused on breathing through my nose, letting him use my mouth. This wasn't Creed seeking a blow job. This was Creed fucking my face both to satisfy his needs and to humiliate me.

I might've defied Creed because I knew it irritated him, but when it came to his pleasure, I was at his beck and call. Always had been. Always would be, despite what had happened between us. Creed was my Alpha; he was the Dominant who owned me, even if he refused to acknowledge it. I would continue to defy him, but I would always be at his mercy.

Creed pulled out of my mouth slowly, pushed back in. Each pump of his hips took him deeper until he was fucking into my throat. Creed was the one who taught me how to control my gag reflex. It was a painstaking process that took time and patience, but it was worth it, even when he fucked my throat raw.

I continued to watch his face, noticing he wouldn't look me in the eye. His attention was on his cock disappearing into my mouth. His jaw was clenched, the muscle bunching as he began to fuck my face faster, harder. His restraint was admirable, even if I felt it slipping more than usual.

The minutes ticked by as he used me. Saliva slid down my chin and neck, my eyes watered, but I didn't make a sound. I was fearful he would stop if he realized I needed this as much as he did. I didn't give a shit that he was using me as a substitute for Journey. I didn't fucking care that he might be thinking about her while he was taking pleasure from me. It didn't matter.

As I submitted to the onslaught, I couldn't help wondering if he remembered the time he made me come during an encounter very much like this one. I wasn't allowed to touch my cock, nor did he provide any stimulation, yet my cock jerked and spurted as though I'd been lodged deep inside a slick, tight pussy. It had been Creed's intention, his desire to see me unhinged from the pleasure I derived from serving him. I knew it would never be possible with anyone else because only this man knew how to give me what I needed, even if I didn't really understand what that was.

The more aggressive he became, the louder he got until he gasped for air, grunting as he fucked my throat.

"Fucking suck me," he barked, pulling out of my throat.

I closed my lips around him and sucked hard, knowing exactly how to pleasure him as he slammed his pelvis into my face, fucking my mouth for all he was worth. I fought my gag reflex, letting him choke me with his cock. The only warning of his impending release was the subtle pulse of his shaft against my lips. When he let go, it was with a satisfied roar, his cock lodged deep in my throat, his cum bypassing my tongue altogether.

And the moment it was over, it was over.

Creed pulled his cock free from my mouth before adjusting his underwear and pulling his jeans up. He didn't even offer a pat on the head before he turned and walked away.

"You are *not* permitted to come," he said, not bothering to look back.

I watched until he disappeared into his room.

Only then did I smile because this side of Creed wasn't one I expected.

I thought I knew him.

Thought I could predict his every move.

Perhaps I'd been able to, but that was before Journey Zeplyn came into our lives.

She had singled-handedly disproven my theory that Creed Granger could not be broken. Without even trying, she had created the first crack in that granite-hard exterior. I had a feeling it was only a matter of time before he broke completely.

Or we all did.

There is more to come for Journey, Creed, Garrison, and Hawk in volume 2, which will be released on February 17, 2023.

ACKNOWLEDGMENTS

I'll start by saying thank you to my husband. Our world has been a bit topsy-turvy as of late, and I know it hasn't been easy for you. As always, you've been my anchor in the storm, even when you were enduring your own chaos, you're always there to ease mine. I don't know what I'd do without you, and I pray I never have to find out.

A big thank you to Chancy Powley for reminding me why I should answer the phone even when I prefer not to. I'm not sure how I got so lucky to have you as a friend, but it means everything that you put up with me the way you do.

A huge shoutout goes to Jenna Underwood. If it wasn't for you, I'm not sure I would've tackled this trope. Although it may not be the traditional reverse harem (if there is such a thing), it's my version, and I'm glad you suggested I go this route.

I also have to thank my street team – Nicole Nation Street Team – Your unwavering support is something I will never take for granted.

Nicole Nation 2.0, for the constant support and love. You've been there for me from almost the beginning. This group of ladies has kept me going for so long, I'm not sure I'd know what to do without them.

And, of course, YOU, the reader. Your emails, messages, posts, comments, tweets… they mean more to me than you can imagine. I thrive on hearing from you, knowing that my characters and my stories have touched you in some way keeps me going. I've been known to shed a tear or two when reading an email because you simply bring so much joy to my life with your support. I thank you for that.

About Nicole Edwards

New York Times and *USA Today* bestselling author Nicole Edwards lives in the suburbs of Austin, Texas, with her husband, their three fur babies, and the youngest of their three children, who has threatened never to leave home. When Nicole is not writing about sexy alpha males and sassy, independent women, she can often be found with a book in hand or attempting to keep the dogs happy. You can find her hanging out on social media and interacting with her readers - even when she's supposed to be writing.

Connect with Nicole

I hope you're as eager to get the information as I am to give it. Any of these things is worth signing up for or feel free to sign up for all. I promise to keep each one unique and interesting.

Nic News: If you haven't signed up for my newsletter and want notifications regarding preorders, new releases, giveaways, sales, etc., then you'll want to sign up. I promise not to spam your email, just get you the most important updates.

Ramblings of a Writer Blog: My blog is used for writer ramblings, which I am known to do from time to time.

NICOLE NATION: Visit my website to get exclusive content you won't find anywhere else, including sneak peeks, A Day in the Life character stories, exclusive giveaways, cards from Nicole, or join Nicole's review team.

NICOLE NATION ON FACEBOOK: Join my reader group to interact with other readers, ask me questions, play fun weekly games, celebrate during release week, and enter exclusive giveaways!

INSTAGRAM: Basically, Instagram is where I post pictures of my dogs, so if you want to see epic cuteness, you should follow me.

TEXT: Want a simple, fast way to get updates on new releases? Sign up for text messaging. If you are in the U.S., simply text NICOLE to 64600. I promise not to spam your phone. This is just my way of letting you know what's happening because I know you're busy, but if you're anything like me, you always have your phone on you.

NAUGHTY & NICE SHOP: Not only does the shop have signed books, but there's fun merchandise, too—plenty of naughty and nice options to go around. Find the shop on my website.

Website:	NicoleEdwards.me
Facebook:	/Author.Nicole.Edwards
Instagram:	NicoleEdwardsAuthor
BookBub:	/NicoleEdwardsAuthor

By Nicole Edwards

THE WALKERS

ALLURING INDULGENCE
Kaleb
Zane
Travis
Holidays with The Walker Brothers
Ethan
Braydon
Sawyer
Brendon

THE WALKERS OF COYOTE RIDGE
Curtis
Jared (a crossover novel)
Hard to Hold
Hard to Handle
Beau
Rex
A Coyote Ridge Christmas
Mack
Kaden & Keegan
Alibi (a crossover novel)
Trey

BRANTLEY WALKER: OFF THE BOOKS
All In
Without A Trace
Hide & Seek
Deadly Coincidence
Alibi (a crossover novel)
Secrets
Confessions
Bounty

Made in the USA
Monee, IL
21 February 2023

28403082R00111